War Song

James Riordan

OXFORD
UNIVERSITY PRESS

For Susan

OXFORD
UNIVERSITY PRESS

Great Clarendon Street, Oxford OX2 6DP

Oxford University Press is a department of the University of Oxford.
It furthers the University's objective of excellence in research, scholarship,
and education by publishing worldwide in

Oxford New York

Athens Auckland Bangkok Bogotá Buenos Aires Calcutta
Cape Town Chennai Dar es Salaam Delhi Florence Hong Kong Istanbul
Karachi Kuala Lumpur Madrid Melbourne Mexico City Mumbai
Nairobi Paris São Paulo Shanghai Singapore Taipei Tokyo Toronto Warsaw

and associated companies in Berlin Ibadan

Oxford is a registered trade mark of Oxford University Press
in the UK and in certain other countries

British Library Cataloguing in Publication Data available

ISBN 0 19 271854 1

1 3 5 7 9 10 8 6 4 2

Typeset by AFS Image Setters Ltd, Glasgow

Printed and bound in Great Britain by
Biddles Ltd, Guildford and King's Lynn

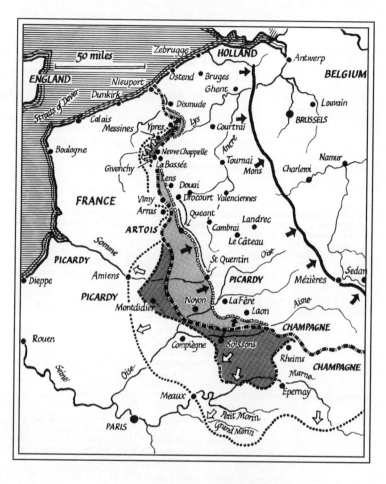

ENGLAND

50 miles

Straits of Dover

Zebrugge

HOLLAND

Antwerp

BELGIUM

Ostend · Bruges

Nieuport

Ghent

Louvain

Dunkirk

Dixmude

BRUSSELS

Calais

Lys

Courtrai

Messines · Ypres

Ancre

Tournai

Namur

Boulogne

Neuve Chappelle

Mons

Charleroi

Givenchy

La Bassée

Lens · Douai

FRANCE

Vimy

Drocourt

Valenciennes

Arras

Queant

Landrec

ARTOIS

Cambrai

Le Câteau

Somme

St Quentin

Oise

Sedan

PICARDY

Amiens

PICARDY

Méziéres

Dieppe

Montdidier

Noyon

La Fère

Laon

CHAMPAGNE

Aisne

PICARDY

Rouen

Compiègne

Soissons

Rheims

CHAMPAGNE

Seine

Oise

Marne

Epernay

Meaux

Petit Morin

PARIS

Grand Morin

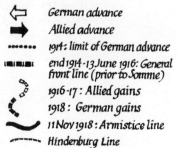

⇦ German advance

➡ Allied advance

••••••• 1914: limit of German advance

▬▬▬ end 1914-13 June 1916: General
front line (prior to Somme)

1916-17 : Allied gains

1918 : German gains

11 Nov 1918 : Armistice line

– – – Hindenburg Line

Prologue

*I realize that patriotism is not enough. I must have
no hatred or bitterness towards anyone.*

Nurse Cavell

At the first grey streak of dawn Pastor le Seur drove to
the Prison of St Gilles. On entering the cell he found the
frail figure kneeling by the bed. A high crown of greying
hair was half covered by the white halo of a nurse's cap,
slightly askew.

A flickering gas flame cast an eerie misshapen
shadow on the stone wall, like a lantern slide of a
monster's child at prayer. Two large bunches of withered
flowers stood drooping in gunmetal vases on the floor,
as at a graveside.

The condemned prisoner had packed all her worldly
possessions in a bag.

'How much time do we have?' she asked without
looking up.

'Less than an hour,' he murmured.

For a fleeting moment a hint of fear showed in the grey
eyes; but it passed swiftly. She pursed her lips and thrust
out her chin.

'May I offer my services . . . as a priest?' he asked.

'No, thank you,' she said with cold politeness.

He tried again, gently, 'Please don't look upon me as
an enemy, rather as God's servant.'

She was silent, uncertain about this prison chaplain.
True, he was a man of God, like her father back home in
Norfolk. But he *had* blessed the German cause . . .

1

Her head took over from her heart: hadn't Christ commanded 'Love thine enemy as thyself'?

'There is one thing . . . '

'I'll do anything in my power.'

'I'd like you to write to my mother. Tell her this: I realize that patriotism is not enough. It isn't enough to love one's own people. I must have no hatred or bitterness towards anyone.'

She spoke as in prayer, her eyes closed, her face upturned. Then, all at once, she rose, picked up her bag and walked briskly from the cell. Quietly and calmly she made her way, as she had through life, down the long gloomy corridor of the great prison.

As she passed the warders and prison officials, a strange thing happened. It was as if Saint Joan of Arc was going to the stake, for they bowed and crossed themselves in awe.

She returned their blessings with dignity, giving each a grateful nod.

In the prison courtyard stood two black motor cars awaiting the two prisoners. First to emerge was the Belgian architect Philippe Baucq, accompanied by a Catholic priest. He walked up to both his guards, shook hands and said, 'Let us bear no grudge.' Then he got into the back of one of the cars, sitting between the two escorts.

A few minutes later the same door swung open and the English nurse stepped on to the wet cobblestones. She walked straight to the car, took her seat, and the two saloons at once moved off. They circled the prison yard before halting at the high spiked gates.

Despite the early hour, a small crowd had gathered outside the prison. Led by deputy matron Elizabeth Wilkins, a party from the nursing school on the rue de la Culture had arrived at 5 a.m. for the very latest news.

2

Would there be an appeal?

A reprieve?

Monsieur Maron, the prison governor, had met them in person. They could tell from his downcast face there was to be no last-minute stay of execution.

'She is being very brave,' he said. 'If you care to wait you will see her when the car emerges.'

So, huddled against the cold drizzle, the band of nurses had waited an hour. At 6 a.m. promptly, the iron gates slowly opened and the two black cars drove quickly through. The onlookers caught no more than a glimpse of their matron in her grey cape and navy blue uniform.

She was sitting bolt upright, staring straight ahead.

That was the last they saw of her.

The two cars sped through the deserted streets, heading for the Tir National, the rifle club two miles from Brussels. On the tarmac of what was now the execution square, a company of two hundred and fifty German soldiers was waiting.

Despite the rain, high-ranking officers in full dress uniform had turned out to oversee formalities: Military Prosecutor Herr Stöber, the Kommandant of St Gilles Captain Behrens, the army doctor Dr Benn, and the Company Commander Colonel Rühl.

Herr Stöber it was who stepped forward to read out the sentence. He was a small dapper man who liked order in everything. Before he could speak, however, a voice cut into the carefully-planned ceremony.

'Comrades, in the presence of death . . . we comrades . . . '

It was young Philippe Baucq. Before he could continue, the guards quickly grabbed his arms and stuffed a rag into his mouth. There would be no further interruptions.

The sentences were read out.

'Mademoiselle Edith Louisa Cavell has been found

guilty of treason—helping English and French soldiers to escape from Belgium. Because of her crime, some two hundred and fifty men joined the Allied Army in Holland. Philippe Baucq was her chief assistant. Both are condemned to death by firing squad on this day, the 12th of October 1915.'

The sentences read out, two priests were permitted to say a last word to the condemned.

Taking the nurse's hand, Pastor le Seur recited the Lord's Prayer. At the 'Amen', she lightly pressed his fingers and murmured, 'Thank you. Please let my loved ones know my soul is safe, and that I am glad to die for my country.'

He took her elbow and led her gently to the wooden post against the far grass verge. A waiting German soldier stood her up against the post and bandaged her eyes. Tears at once wet the bandage and trickled down beneath the sightless eyes.

The slim woman, her hair held in a bun by two metal combs, her jaw set defiantly forward, calmly awaited the moment of death.

She made no sound as two parties of eight riflemen were marched forward to a line six paces from the execution posts. At a sharp command from the officer, they raised the rifles to their shoulders. Almost at once came a second command:

'FIRE!'

Two volleys rang out and both figures sank to the ground without a sound. No scream, no cry for mercy.

Pastor le Seur muffled a cry of horror. He had never witnessed an execution before, let alone that of a woman. Nurse Cavell had slumped forward; three times she seemed to try to rise. Blood was pouring from her face.

He later learned from the doctor that the jerking of her body was merely a reflex action. For as he and Dr Benn ran forward, they saw that the bullet holes were as large as a fist and went right through her body. One bullet had smashed her lower jaw and her head was now lying in a rapidly filling pool of blood.

It was done.

The doctor certified death and, a few minutes later, two coffins were lowered into newly-dug graves.

So died one of England's noblest heroines.

1

I'm war. Remember me?
'Yes, you're asleep,' you say, 'and you kill men,'
Look in my game-bag, fuller than you think . . .

I kill families.
Cut off the roots, the plant will root no more . . .

I am the game that nobody can win.
What's yours is mine, what's mine is still my own.
I'm War. Remember me.
                    from 'Achtung! Achtung!' by Mary Hacker

Like the girls in her class, Florence and Dorothy Loveless
had sat silent beside the schoolmistress, arms folded,
backs straight, while Miss Harmer had read out the nurse's
story. For a full minute the room of seventy girls was
deathly quiet—apart from a few sniffles and sobs.

Miss Harmer herself, normally stern of stare and cold
of demeanour was having trouble with a heaving chest.

Finally, with a humph-humph cough to clear her throat,
she put down the Cavell story and pulled herself together.

'Is there nothing the beastly Germans won't do?' she
flung at the class, and her two helpers, the Loveless girls,
as if they knew the answer. 'To murder a poor English
nurse in cold blood, I ask you . . . '

There was a lesson to be learned here, and the
schoolmarm was not one to let it slip.

'Let the noble sacrifice of Nurse Cavell be an example
to you all. At Christmastide you girls will be leaving

school to take your places in the world. Help the war effort and avenge the nurse's death—that's my advice to you. War opens up new horizons. Before the war, many of you would have gone into domestic service at half a crown a week. Now, look, you can do factory work for good pay, making shells and guns, bullets and bombs.'

Recalling a song she'd heard recently, Miss Harmer began to write neatly on the blackboard. Uplifted by the stirring words, she got the entire class to chant the answer to her question:

'Girls, what can you be?'

'The Girl Behind the Man Behind the Gun.'

'Once more.'

'The Girl Behind the Man Behind the Gun.'

'Well done, class. Now copy it into your exercise books.'

Seventy pen nibs dipped into thirty-five inkwells and wrote scratchily on lined paper:

'We are the girls behind the men behind the guns.'

Despite this heart-pounding 'call to arms', Miss Harmer now had to move on to the next lesson of the day— housewifery. While the boys at George Street Elementary School did woodwork, the girls donned white pinafores and trooped out of the school building to the model house next door.

There they learned to sweep, dust, polish, cook, wash, iron, make beds, and bathe a life-sized doll.

Most of them were dab hands at those chores already.

'Munitionettes, not cooks and sweeps, are what we need to win the war,' Miss Harmer muttered to her helpers. She had dared to mention it once to the headmaster, Mr Cleal; but he would have none of it.

'A woman's place is in the home,' he insisted.

He even looked down his nose at women teachers. But, as he grumbled to his wife, 'Needs must where the Devil drives.'

Not that the George Street girls minded doing housewifery. They were accustomed to their place in school life. To protect them from the 'rough boys', they had separate classes, separate playgrounds, even a separate entrance. 'GIRLS' was carved in stone above the door.

Too bad for the boys. Housewifery was far more fun than boring old woodwork. When the teacher's back was turned, the girls jumped on the beds, had pillow fights, splashed each other from the chipped enamel tubs, swept dirt under the mats, and drowned the hated doll.

The boys didn't know what they were missing.

On their way home from school that afternoon, the twins Florence and Dorothy still had the nurse story stuck in their heads.

'I wouldn't mind being a nurse,' said Floss.

'Garn, nursing ain't for the likes of us,' retorted Doss. 'That Cavell was a vicar's daughter with pots of dosh.'

'That's as maybe . . . But this time last year we could've been dusting for two measly bob a week. Now we can do a "man's" job for three quid. Makes you think, dunnit?'

'Beats dressmaking,' said Doss. 'I was promised one and six a week, eight to eight. Long hours for nuffink.'

'Well, now's our chance. What with our Jack and Dad and the rest of 'em fighting and dying, there'll soon be only women left.'

They marched on, their two younger sisters and brother in tow, each dreaming of adventure and riches beyond their wildest dreams.

They were right to dream. In the scorching summer of 1914, there had been no hint that the world was about to be turned upside-down—or that, for many, it was about to end altogether.

Now, at the end of 1916, two-thirds of Europe was alight and the flames were licking out towards the whole world. Already half the youth of half the world, like moths to a flame, had been drawn into a war that raged across the muddy fields of France and Belgium—where Jack was fighting—and among the blinding sandstorms of Palestine—where Dad was posted.

The 'gallant British Army' that had routed Napoleon at Waterloo, tamed the Russian Bear in the Crimea, singed Boer beards in South Africa, and won an Empire that stretched all round the globe . . . was bogged down on the Somme, and suffering untold losses.

Girls were badly needed on the home front: to drive trams, trucks, and trains, as brickies and chippies, as miners and munition workers. For some it was as exciting as a boy's running away to sea. Now, for the first time, they could earn enough to keep themselves, get away from home. No longer did they have to bow and scrape to tyrants in country homes.

'We're 'ome, Mum,' yelled the twins together as they pushed through the open front door of 39 George Street.

'Shush,' came a muffled voice from the scullery. 'You'll wake up Joey.'

A wail from the parlour soon greeted them. Joey was awake.

'Oh well, he'll have to air 'is tonsils,' muttered Mrs Loveless. 'I've only one pair of 'ands.'

It was washday.

Wearing a coarse apron of sacking and a square of oilskin across her chest, she was rubbing each item with her Sunlight soap, giving extra elbow grease to the wee and poo stains. After she'd done the whites, she tossed them into the copper together with a shower of soda, stirring the boiling bundle with her copper stick.

The whole place reeked of steamy washing.

After a good soaking, she lifted the washing out and left it to drain as she struggled to the sink with the dirty water. Having emptied it down the sink, she refilled the tub with cold water and placed it under the wringer. Then she rinsed the washing once and put it through the wooden rollers, turning the mangle handle with her free hand.

If the weather had been fine she'd have hung the whole lot out to dry. But since it was raining, she had to string it up on a clothes line indoors, so that it flapped about their heads in the cramped kitchen and parlour.

To each of the kids she gave a task. To the youngest— Reggie, the younger twins, and Timmie—sweeping the kitchen, scullery, and passage; to the eldest—Elsie, Annie, Floss, and Doss—cleaning the grate and making a fire with newspaper, sticks, and coke. That gave her a breather for changing Joey's nappy and getting tea for the ten of them—bread, marge, and plum jam.

With four infants to mind, she could have done with the twins at home rather than them spending an extra couple of years as school helpers. Like other children, they'd left school at 12, but gone back to lend a hand for a few pennies a week. She would really have had them earning real cash at a man's job; it was hard to manage on her soldiers' allowance.

Still, she thought, I shouldn't grumble. At least our Bert and Jack are safe (touch wood!), unlike Jack's mates Harry and Freddy, and poor Mr Garside opposite.

As she sat down for fifteen minutes, she fished out Jack's last letter, holding it in one hand as she spooned bread and milk into Joey's mouth with the other.

And she cried.

Not at her own hard lot. But at the war.

It was no longer somewhere over there, out of sight. It was on the doorstep. It wasn't just the soldiers on crutches that had brought home the horrors of war. Every day, in column after column, the casualty lists filled whole pages of newspapers. The army that had first crossed the Channel in the autumn of 1914, Jack and Harry among them, was by now practically wiped out.

Yet they still called for more.

'Join Up, Join Up, Join Up!' was the cry.

Recruiting posters bawled from every billboard:

'Women of Britain Say—Go!'

Had anyone ever asked them?

2

Ev'rybody's doing
Something for the War,
Girls are doing things
They've never done before,
Go as bus conductors,
Drive a car or van,
All the world is topsy-turvy
Since the War began.
from 'Sing a Song of War-time' by Nina Macdonald

The twins couldn't wait to do their bit. But *what* bit was it to be? Luckily, they had Mr Cleal, the headmaster, to help them in their choice.

On their last day as school helpers, they stood on the platform listening to Mr Cleal addressing his girls. No one was more surprised than *his girls*. Normally, his rousing send-offs were reserved for boys alone, future fathers of nation and Empire. Never a word for the nation's future mothers.

Yet on this Friday morning in December, Mr Cleal was thinking of 'his' girls; it was his duty to set them on the right path.

As he swept into the school hall for morning assembly, his dumpy figure draped in a black gown, he gave sure sign of fire and brimstone to come. The gown billowed out dustily behind him as he marched briskly up to the platform, mounted the steps and took his place at the lectern, glaring about him.

While waiting for the usual coughs and wheezes to die

down, he smoothed back his few remaining wisps of ginger hair, adjusted his glasses, and gripped the lectern hard with both hands.

To his dismay, no former boys or masters had been killed in action that week—so he was denied the chance to treat school to another tub-thumping speech followed by a full-throated 'Abide With Me'. All the same, he clearly wished to get something off his chest. He couldn't wait for total silence.

'Quiet!' he roared impatiently.

That did the trick.

'The war goes on,' he began solemnly in a low voice. 'Many a gallant lad has laid down his life for King and Country. Some of our own George Street boys are among the noble heroes journeying to Valhalla . . . '

The children sitting cross-legged before him on the wooden floor naturally thought Valhalla was another battle site, like Ypres or Mons.

'Harry Newell, Frederick Feltham, Mr Holyoake . . . '

Merely to list their names made old Ginger's eyes water.

'School honours their memory.'

He gazed round the hall hopefully at his boys and girls.

'Someone must fill the gaps as heroes fall. On the battle front and' (long pause) ' . . . on the *home* front.'

He sighed and shifted position so that he stood side on to the female half of the hall. The fidgety squatters were expecting yet another call to 'keep the home fires burning'.

'Now then, girls . . . '

He swept them with a gaze rather like that of a football captain picking sides and faced with the last two fatties.

'When lads answer the call to arms, somebody has to do their jobs. That is where you girls step into the breach, do your bit for the duration.'

There, it was out. He didn't like it. But it needed to be said. It was the Head's duty to make tough decisions, show a lead. With a scowl and voice rising to the rafters, he yelled, 'You girls must take your place. But you must also *know your place*. When our gallant boys come marching home, you will return to your proper role—darning socks and making dumplings.'

He was now working up a head of steam, like a train gathering speed. Suddenly, his face grew red and, as usual when he mounted his latest hobby horse, no one knew what he was on about.

'Do not heed the siren calls of those brazen hussies—the Suffragettes. They are the enemy within, the Hun in our midst. They burn down houses, throw stones and axes, slash precious paintings, defy law and order. Why, one harpy even tried to bring down His Majesty's horse in the Epsom Derby.

'They will stop at nothing to gain the vote for women. Just imagine what that could lead to—petticoat government!'

The picture of the Prime Minister Mr Lloyd George in petticoat, brassiere, and corsets brought a grin to several faces and a loud guffaw from Mr Jeffries, the PT master standing behind the Head. But his face soon changed as Mr Cleal squawked, 'Stop that sniggering! This is deadly serious. Nature made men and women different.' (More giggles in the hall.) 'By nature man is the doer, the creator, the discoverer, defender of the home. His energy is for adventure, for war, for conquest. Men like Nelson, Drake, Newton, Brunel, Kitchener . . . Girls were born with different gifts. Their spirit is too weak and gentle for politics and adventure. Their place is in the home, as loyal wives and mothers.'

The two schoolmarms shifted uneasily as the eyes of the children moved from Mr Cleal to them: why were

14

they not home right now, darning socks and cooking dumplings?

Mr Cleal was coming to a triumphant finale. One last patriotic thump on the lectern drum.

'So go forth, school. Put your fingers in the dyke, plug the gaps in workers' ranks, all hands to the dockyard pumps. *But* . . . remember: with England's victory over the Hun, you girls will return to your rightful places in the home! Let us praise the Lord for our gallant men.'

With a nod to Mrs Modyford at the piano, he handed over the hymn singing to staff and pupils.

> 'Onward Christian soldiers, marching as to war,
> With the cross of Jesus going on before . . . '

That evening, when they were having tea round the kitchen table, Floss asked her mother a question. It had been bothering her all day, like a fishbone in the gullet.

'Mum, what's a sufferajit?'

Mum gave her an odd look, switched Joey from left to right arm, and frowned.

'Wha'? You mean Suffragette? Now, who's been putting ideas into your head?'

'Mr Cleal, Mum.'

'Oh, I see, has he now? Well, he's the last person I'd expect to talk of Suffragettes. What was he on about?'

'He called them brazen hussies because they want women to have the vote so's the Prime Minister can wear petticoats.'

Mrs Loveless gave a weary smile.

'Well, he would, wouldn't he? He's a man. But he's right on one thing: them Suffragettes want the vote for women, same as men.'

'Wha' for?' asked Doss. 'Waste of time if you ask me.'

'Well, love, that's the trouble, isn't it? Nobody does ask you because you're a woman. Do they ask *us* if we

15

want a war? Did they ask Nurse Cavell whether *she* wanted to get shot?'

'But Mr Cleal said nature made us different. Women are too weak for politics.'

Mrs Loveless snorted.

'Is a male drunk or loony better qualified to vote than a woman teacher or factory hand, even Queen Mary for that matter?'

The twins stared into the fire. Thoughts of votes and loonies, queens and nurses were all jumbled up with 'doing their bit for the duration'—whatever that meant.

A glance at the gaunt, ageing, shapeless figure of their mother, exhausted by ten kids, told them something else.

War offered them a chance to make something of their lives.

3

'Fight the year out!' the War-lords said:
What said the dying among the dead?

'To the last man!' cried the profiteers:
What said the poor in the starveling years?

'War is good!' yelled the Jingo-kind:
What said the wounded, the maimed and blind?

'Fight on!' the Armament-kings besought:
Nobody asked what the women thought.
From 'A Fight to a Finish' by S. Gertrude Ford

It was a bleak Christmas. What with two places empty at the table and no news of Dad in six weeks, the mood was far from festive. True, they had decorated the parlour with paper chains they'd cut, painted, and stuck together with flour paste.

But the Loveless family couldn't afford a Christmas tree and each evening they sat in the half-dark to save on gas.

Jack's last letter made gloomy reading: his platoon had advanced no more than the length of a football pitch in the last eighteen months. Yet how much blood, flesh, and bones had been trampled into that pitiful square of mud!

The war had gone to earth and neither side could dislodge the other from the trenches. A strip of murdered nature stretched from the North Sea all the way to the Swiss border.

What was the point of it all? Wrecks of one-legged men hung about aimlessly on street corners, staring at sights only they could see.

More and more people were protesting. What *was* the war about? Was it not a war between governments, not ordinary people, let alone women? The rich were growing fat on vast war profits, while armchair tub-thumpers prattled on about The Supreme Sacrifice. Newspapers lied about the fighting and the Top Brass lived in clover while planning battles at a front they never saw.

It was mainly women, soldiers' wives and mothers, who led the protests—and largely men who pelted them with rotten fruit, tore down their banners, and drowned their chants with patriotic songs.

But there were more pressing issues that bothered the Loveless family. Food was scarce. What with Jerry boats sinking British food ships, it was getting harder to put grub on the table—meat and potatoes, tea and sugar, margarine and butter. And you had to queue for hours. Not only that, the price of food had doubled since the start of the Great War.

For Mrs Loveless, mealtimes became a massive headache with nine hungry mouths to feed. It broke her heart to kill and skin Jack's rabbits, but the family had to eat something. Just recently, she had been able to buy cheap hot meals from the new 'cost-price' restaurant that Mrs Pankhurst's Women's Social and Political Union had set up. But they were living on a shoestring; and the string was frayed and stretched to breaking point.

What made matters worse was the rent. Ever since extra dockers had been pouring into Portsmouth, landlords had been jacking up rents. It was the issue that drew the Loveless family willy-nilly into the women's struggle.

Mr Wallace—'Ebenezer' to his tenants, after Ebenezer Scrooge—owned most of the houses in George Street, as well as the sidestreets all about. As regular as clockwork, he would come knocking of a Friday teatime, holding out his bony hand and ticking off paid rents in his little black book. Sometimes families would hide out the back, but there was always a baby's yell to give them away; sooner or later they had to open the front door to the grim-faced man in his shiny black suit, with his brown pipe stuck in his mouth like a rotting tooth.

When Mrs Loveless opened up on Christmas Eve, with Joey perched on her right hip, she had the eight and sixpence ready in her thin red hand. She was most particular about paying bills, scared stiff of falling into debt. To scrape the rent together she'd had to pawn Jack's old bike and her gold wedding ring.

'Here y'are, you old skinflint,' she said. 'Eight and six to the last farthing.'

Names never bothered Mr Wallace. Money did.

'Ten bob this week, missus,' he said as if stating a well-known fact, like 'It's Christmas' or 'water's wet'.

Mrs Loveless stared at him aghast. Fear gripped her innards and squeezed till the pips squeaked.

'You can't!' she gasped. 'I ain't got ten bob.'

'Take in a lodger then. There's plenty of young gals needing a roof over their heads.'

'With nine kids?! Where'll they sleep—in the lav?'

'That's your look-out, missus,' he said, puffing calmly on his extra tooth.

He still took the three half crowns and shilling held out to him, dropped the coins in his leather bag and entered the debt into his rent book.

19

'I'll be back next week for what I'm due,' he muttered, moving on to next door's knocker.

Half an hour later, Mrs Jones from next door stomped into the Loveless kitchen.

'What's to do, Maisie?' she asked. 'It's the third rent rise this year. I can't afford it.'

'Well, he can't get blood out of a stone, Iris.'

'No, but he can chuck us out, babes and all.'

The two women stared gloomily at the cracked and faded oilskin cloth on the kitchen table, shaking their heads.

'Our Flossie was talking 'bout some ladies in the Women's Housing Association planning a rent strike down Fratton way. If people stick together and refuse to pay, the landlords'll have to give in.'

'What? Don't you believe it. They've got the police, courts, and government on their side; they'd turf us out and find us another home—in jug!'

'I tell you this though, Iris, I'm skint. They'll *have* to put me inside. Then what'll become of the kids?'

Iris thumped her fist on the table in a sudden spurt of anger.

'We *must* do summat! Maybe it's worth getting in touch with this Women's Housing Association? What've we got to lose?'

Three days later, on Monday evening, a dozen women packed into the dingy parlour of No. 39 to hear a Mrs Julia Huxley. Although the local women were wary of this 'outsider' with her airs and graces, they had no one else to turn to. At least she seemed to be on their side.

'Refuse to pay,' she said abruptly. 'Start a rent strike. Other girls have done it. Last year as many as a hundred and fifty thousand up in Glasgow went on strike. And they won. As a result, the government passed an act to stop landlords putting up rents. So now it's illegal. If we stand together we'll win too.'

It was agreed—though few had much hope of success. But what else could they do?

The George Street women refused to pay the rent rise. To their surprise, more and more streets joined in; soon the whole of Buckland had backed the strike. None of them had ever defied the law before. But, then, this was *war* in the midst of war . . .

The landlords hit back: right away they got court leave to evict the strikers. But that was easier said than done. Under Mrs Huxley's guidance, the women prepared a plan of action.

At both ends of the street, sentries sat outside the houses, watching for the bailiff. As soon as he appeared, a bell rang and women came running from all the houses, some floury if baking, some wet with soap suds if washing. They came armed with rotten fruit to hurl, rolling pins to biff, and toasting forks to stick up bottoms.

Each time the poor man had to flee for his life, chased by a mob of angry women.

All was quiet for a week or so. Then, late one evening at the start of the New Year, Black Marias descended like hungry crows and rent strikers were bundled off to jail. Mostly the coppers nabbed younger women, those without a family to support.

Next day, eighteen young women went on trial at the law courts on Guildhall Square. For 'breach of the peace'. Among them was fifteen-year-old Florence Loveless.

As Floss stood nervously in the dock, wondering if her first job would be picking oakum from old rope in jail, she suddenly heard shouts, chanting, and singing from outside.

Thousands were pouring into the square.

The noise caused bedlam inside the crowded courtroom. The three magistrates went into a huddle, hummed and hawed, peered through the grimy windows and then hastily announced their decision.

'Case dropped. You are free to go.'

Later Floss discovered the reason. The Women's Housing Association had persuaded dockyard munition workers to stop work for a day and march to court with the rent strikers. As many as ten thousand people turned up.

When the eighteen heroines appeared, they were cheered and chaired through the streets. Mrs Loveless felt as proud of her daughter as she did of her son and husband. All three were fighting a just battle in the war.

The case was dropped and the landlords were fined for putting up rents. The women had won.

It was a lesson in solidarity not lost on the twins as they went to sign on for work.

4

She's the girl that makes the thing
That drills the hole, that holds the spring
That drives the rod, that turns the knob
That works the thingummybob.
It's a ticklish sort of job
Making a thing for a thingummybob
Especially when you don't know what it's for.
And it's the girl that makes the thing
That holds the oil that oils the ring
That makes the thingummybob that's going to win the
*   war.*

Anon.

With Mum in need of every brass farthing, the twins had to get a better-paid job. They were now fifteen and big for their age—'going on twenty', as Gran never stopped saying.

Although they were both tall and raw-boned, with thick dark hair and brown deep-set eyes, there the similarity ended. Dorothy was the prettier of the two, with a winning smile and the sort of natural grace that attracted wolf whistles from men on building sites. And she played up to it, swinging her hips and sticking out her shapely bosom.

Everything about Florence seemed made a size too big. Her long-fingered hands were strong and muscular like a navvy's mitts; her big feet took twice as big a stride as those of her sister; she had a wide, full-lipped mouth, square, slightly-dimpled chin, and long hawk-like nose.

In temperament, too, the girls were near opposites.

Whereas Dorothy's mood was as changeable as the weather, depending on what side of the bed she got out of that morning—full of beans one moment, flat as a pancake the next, Florence was the serious one, her head forever stuck in books or women's papers like *The Suffragette*, *Britannia*, or *Dreadnought*. She didn't fly off the handle like Doss; though awkward in movement and company, she was more calm, thoughtful, and caring. It was Floss who performed the family duty of replying to the war letters, always digging up news for Jack and Dad. Doss would spend more time chewing the pencil end than writing.

When it came to hard work, the twins had already mastered all the household chores. Being the eldest girls, they had been expected since the age of twelve to run the home whenever Mum was 'in confinement' or otherwise unwell.

Now they were taking what 'Gingernob' Cleal called their 'first step on the road to life'. True, the recruitment leaflets for women workers addressed themselves to those 'between the ages of 18 and 35'. But the dockyard was so short of hands the twins weren't expecting any argy-bargy over age.

Besides gobbling up thousands of men, the deep throat of war had already swallowed up millions upon millions of shells, far more than had been planned in 1914. So the government had turned hundreds of factories over to making shells and guns; and now they needed several hundred thousand women to 'man' them.

They couldn't be choosy about sex and age. It was the same with many other jobs, from chimney sweep to farm labourer. The 'weaker sex' had to turn their hand to everything—besides running the home and bringing up a family.

On a crisp Monday morning in mid-January, the twins walked the two miles to the Labour Exchange in Lake

Road. Already a chattering band of girls and older women was hanging about outside, noses pressed against the window, studying recruitment posters and postcard ads.

The poster that caught Doss's eye called for 'Women munition workers' to 'Enrol at once'. It featured a smiling young woman clad in overalls, pulling on her cap over dark short-cut hair. In the background was a huge trench gun firing across barbed wire. The poster proclaimed in bold letters:

'ON HER Their Lives Depend'

'Well, well, that's a turn-up for the book,' someone muttered. 'Now they need us, they say lives depend on us. What's a life worth, that's what I'd like to know. How much are they paying?'

Floss's gaze was fixed on a poster of three nurses standing before a list of possible destinations: France, Italy, Holland, Russia, Egypt, Mesopotamia . . . At the bottom of the poster was the word 'VAD' in big letters and a list of jobs:

'Nursing members, cooks, kitchen maids, house maids, laundresses, ward maids, motor drivers, etc. ARE URGENTLY NEEDED.'

Whatever VAD stood for, Floss knew she could cope with all the maid's jobs—though they weren't her idea of nursing.

After half an hour of queueing, the twins found themselves summoned to Table No. 12. A score of trestle tables were scattered around the old drill hall ready for interviews. The white-haired man across the table was holding a pencil in one hand and a cigarette in the other; before him was a white form. He was evidently hoping to kill two birds with one form.

'Right, young ladies, first I'll take down your particulars, as the actress said to the bishop.'

25

It was a joke he'd already made a dozen times that morning. Since they hadn't thought of becoming an actress or a bishop, the smart alec joke was completely lost on the twins.

Name, date of birth, nationality, address, school, health record, certificates, previous work experience, were all dealt with swiftly.

'So what do you fancy?' he asked brightly, squinting up at them through a cloud of mauve tobacco smoke.

'What pays best?' asked Dorothy bluntly. In case that sounded too forward, she thought she'd better add, 'Our family's hard up.'

'Aren't they all,' he said wearily. He clucked his tongue like an old hen. 'Where's your patriotic spirit? I don't understand you girls these days. Still, if you're not afraid of hard work, how about munitions?'

'What's that exactly?' they asked.

'You know, stuffing gunpowder into shells—"stemming" they calls it.'

'Isn't that dangerous?' asked Doss.

'Not as dangerous as firing the blooming things,' he remarked with a wry smile. 'Yeah, it can be dodgy. Tough too: twelve-hour shifts, one day off a week. It's the army's first line, making shells that make the war. "Tommy's sister" they calls it. But if you girls want something more cushy . . .'

'How much?' persisted Doss.

'Free uniform. Three quid a week, almost as much as men get, you lucky devils.'

Doss didn't hesitate.

'Sign me up.'

Three pounds was a tidy old sum—nearly three months' rent. Mum would be pleased.

'You, too, gal?'

'What else is there?' asked Floss uncertainly.

'Sky's the limit. There's a war on. You can help run trains and trams, become a Bobby—or Betty in your case—maintaining law and order in the Women's Police Force, keep the wheels of industry turning. Anything you like.'

'How about nursing? Can I be a VAD?'

His cheery grin faded. 'Not for the likes of you, my gal.'

Floss's face fell. 'Why not?'

'Well, first you've got to be 19 minimum, 23 to go overseas. Now *we* can bend the rules a weeny bit on age, but you'd never fool those geezers on the nursing board. And second, you're not really cut out for VADs—the Voluntary Aid Detachment. See, "voluntary" is a fancy word for "unpaid". True, the government's just doled out twenty quid a year, but with that you've got to buy your own togs and other bits and pieces.' He shrugged his shoulders. 'Nah, leave the nursing lark to dames like Flo Nightingale and Edie Cavell.'

Floss wasn't to be put off. 'I've got my First Aid Certificate,' she said, pulling the paper from her pocket.

His look turned sour. 'Oh, good, so you knows how to make beds and beef tea, eh? Maybe dress cuts and grazes. Listen, girlie, forget the old "ministering angel" gubbins. Shall I tell you what war nursing is?'

He was bent on flushing it out of her system.

'You work in a flooded operating theatre somewhere in Flanders, where four ops are going on at one time and as many as ten amputations an hour. You nurse men with terrible wounds and lay them out when they croak. You nurse in wards that stink of gangrene. You nurse men choking to death as the fluid rises in their gassed lungs, men whose faces are mutilated beyond recognition, whose bodies are mangled beyond repair, whose nerves are shattered beyond healing. That's nursing for you. Could *you* do that?'

Floss had turned pale. She couldn't answer truthfully
. . . Then she thought of Jack. What if he badly needed
nursing?

'I don't rightly know,' she murmured. 'But I'd like to
try.'

'Come on, Flossie,' broke in Doss, 'let's work together.
Just think how pleased Mum'll be with the money, and to
know we're both safe.'

Floss sighed. 'All right, put me down for munitions.
But I *will* be a nurse one day, you'll see.'

'That's the spirit,' exclaimed the clerk. 'Stick to your
guns, gal. But for now, report to the dockyard sorting office
at eight tomorrow morning. Best of luck to the pair of
you.'

So that was it. The Big Adventure. Crossing the bridge
from child to adult. What was life like in the big grown-up
world of work?

5

The guns out there are roaring fast, the bullets fly like
*   rain;*
The aeroplanes are curvetting, they go and come again;
The bombs talk loud; the mines crash out; no trench
*   their might withstands.*
Who helped them all to do their job? The girls with
*   yellow hands.*

The boys out there have hands of red; it's German
*   blood, and warm.*
The Germans know what's coming when the English
*   swarm—*
Canadians and British, and the men from southern
*   lands.*
Who helped them all to do their job? The girls with
*   yellow hands.*

from 'The Girls with Yellow Hands' sung by workers
in an explosives factory in Kent

Mrs Loveless fussed over her new workhands like a mother
cat about to lose her kittens. She washed and brushed their
hair, spruced them up, kissed and caressed them. And
when they left to catch the tram, she sank down in the
armchair, put her head in her hands and cried.

'My babies, my babies!' she sobbed.

Of course, they had to fly the nest sometime.

Of course, she badly needed the extra cash.

Of course, it was wartime and everyone had to do their
bit.

The more shells were made, the more Germans would be killed, the quicker the war would be over, the sooner Jack and Bert would come home.

That was really it. The source of the waterworks went deeper: her nagging worry about Bert. Although he wasn't one for writing regularly, he always sent a standard card or letter each month without fail.

It was now nine weeks and three days since he last wrote!

At every knock on the door, Maisie Loveless leapt a mile, touched the nearest piece of wood for luck and dragged her feet up the passage in dread of the telegram boy. Apart from that odd time when news of Leo Garside opposite had gone to No. 39 instead of No. 38, the Angel of Death had not yet come calling.

Without the twins for support, she would now have to face the ordeal alone. Pray God it wasn't today, tomorrow, or any day.

Meanwhile, on the packed tram the twins were dismayed to find themselves the butt of men's jibes. The moment Floss had stated their destination: 'Dockyard, please; two fares,' heads had turned their way.

As they went to move down the tram, a burly fellow in a grubby boilersuit blocked their way. Despite their 'Excuse me, mister,' he refused to budge. But they tricked him. As Doss went to squeeze by on one side, Floss slipped past on the other. That really got up his nose.

'Filching men's jobs are you, you little vixen. At half our wage I wouldn't bet! You're scabs, blacklegs, that's what you are!'

Other dockers on the tram growled agreement and joined in the taunts.

'Go home and darn your stockings, you flappers!'

'What's a flapper, Floss?' whispered Dossie.

'I guess they mean a girl who doesn't do as she's told—by men.'

As the twins and a few older women went to get off at the dockyard gates, they were pushed and hustled. One beefy middle-aged woman gave as good as she got, digging the jostlers in the midriff with her umbrella.

'Take a stout sharp-pointed brolly with you tomorrow,' she advised the girls.

Male envy didn't end at the tram terminus. Taunts followed women workers all the way to the dockyard sorting office.

'Pay no notice,' said the umbrella woman. 'Poor little dears, they're scared we'll pinch their jobs after the war.'

'Yeah, and that we'll be wearing the trousers,' added another woman.

'Well, they'll have to lump it,' came an Irish voice. 'Ask them why they aren't at the front; that'll trim their sails.'

And she bawled out in a strong voice as they marched through the dockyard gates:

'We don't want to lose you, but we think you ought to go,
For your King and your country both need you so.
We shall want you and miss you,
But with all our might and main,
We shall cheer you, thank you, kiss you,
When you come back home again.'

At the sorting office, the twins were issued with number discs, 167 and 168, and directed to Munitions Workshop No. 5. They were to report to a Mrs Harriet Harcourt, the Lady Welfare Supervisor. With a ragged line of other women, they trudged down cinder paths, counting off the munitions workshops until they reached Number Five.

The supervisor was waiting for them. What a formidable figure! Huge and shapeless like a great sack of nutty slack, her vast frame was draped in a khaki and scarlet smock tied in the middle by a black canvas belt. Over her smoothed-back black hair was a hooded cloak and on her feet was a pair of brown canvas shoes.

She seemed to speak only in booming foghorn tones.

'Listen here! I hire and fire all female labour, got it? I keep order and discipline at work, right? I tell you how to dress and behave. You do as I say.'

She swept them all with her hooded eyes, like a mother eagle surveying her brood.

'You will be searched each time you enter the workshop. Anyone found with the tiniest scrap of metal or matches will go straight to prison, understand? Anyone late or missing work without my say-so gets fined. Right? You day shift workers clock on at 6.20 a.m. and finish at 6.20 p.m., then hand over to the nightshift . . . unless there's overtime. Sundays are free time. Now, get your safety clothing from the stores and be back here pronto. Get cracking!'

Soon all the women were done up in khaki and scarlet like Mrs Ha-Ha, as someone dubbed her from the first two letters of her name.

They shuffled over the dressing room lino in their canvas shoes. Two policewomen searched them thoroughly, then led the way through the double workshop door.

The twins were shocked at their first sight and sound of a factory floor. The noise was deafening, the air was full of choking, stinking fumes, and the vast windowless hangar was freezing cold. *This* was where they'd have to work twelve hours non-stop, six days a week from dawn to dusk?

Beside a moving conveyor belt stood a long line of women, filling cigar-shaped shells as high as their waist. At the side of each shellcase stood a tub of greyish-white powder that was being rammed into the case with a stick

32

and wooden mallet. When it seemed the shell was full, the women took a long thin stem and hammered a small hole in the packed powder. Into this hole they inserted more powder.

Again and again and again.

The twins were fascinated by this job of work. Not so much by the excitement of the new-fangled experience as by the sheer monotony of doing one and the same motion over and over.

If this is what men did in peace time, they could keep it! But, then, it wasn't the work, it was what it earned; and, as they were to discover, the company of other women.

There was something else that caught their attention.

Some of the women's skins and fringes were bright yellow!

Seeing the shocked looks, Mrs Ha-Ha bellowed above the din, 'The shells are filled with TNT. It's a poisonous substance used in making explosives. Although we wear protective clothing, I must warn you that long exposure to TNT turns your skin and hair yellow. Take care and it won't harm you, the colour wears off by itself.'

Her words only served to furrow brows and narrow eyes.

'You run risks like soldiers at the front,' she boomed. 'Yellow is our badge of pride. You're now a Canary Girl.'

The women could think of better names, but they kept them to themselves.

6

Washing up the dishes;
  Washing up the plates;
Washing up the greasy tins,
  That everybody hates.

Scouring out the buckets;
  Cleaning down the stoves.
Guess I'm going to 'stick it',
  Though my fancy roves.

Others are much smarter;
  More clever, too, than I.
Still I go on 'charing';
  Singing cheerfully—
from 'VAD Scullery-maid's Song' by
M. Winifred Wedgwood

The twins found themselves in a team of ten including
four novices. The older hands soon showed them the
ropes, jollied them along with songs and smutty jokes that
burned their tender ears. At break-time, the older women
let off steam by dancing in the yard, linking arms and
kicking up their legs.

Sometimes a girl would read out a much-thumbed
letter; and there'd be a respectful hush as they all thought
of loved ones far away.

Doss took to the job like a pig to muck. She loved
factory life, mixing with hundreds of other women in a
vast building like a cathedral—so different from the

34

cramped space at home, with kids always under your feet. The women relied on one another, helped each other out, knowing that one slip or shoddy job could mean curtains for them all.

Most of all, Doss felt proud to do her bit for the war, even if it was a bit dodgy. And if she turned the colour of a canary, never mind, she would sing like a canary too and enjoy life while she could. On her day off she'd sally forth and have a fine old time in dance rooms or the local pub, with shortened skirt, bobbed hair, and even a Woodbine sticking out of her mouth.

She felt so daring . . . and free.

Not so Floss. She was increasingly troubled by munitions work. She was now part of the war, a cog in the war machine. She was making shells—'the girl behind the man behind the gun'—that blew men to smithereens.

Her fellow workers didn't seem to share her qualms.

On Sundays, as if to ease her conscience, Floss took a part-time job scrubbing floors at the Royal Hospital. It seemed the closest she would come to nursing. Her fellow 'scrubber' was an older, mid-twenty-something woman who didn't seem to know one end of a scrubbing brush from the other. She was glad of Floss's help.

From the woman's uniform, it was clear she was a VAD nurse. She wore a close-fitting grey bonnet tied with white strings under her chin, with a tail hanging down the back. The smart mauve and white check, ankle-length dress was covered with a short scarlet cape which, as she told Floss, 'was specially designed by Florence Nightingale to conceal female curves from the eyes of dirty old men'.

Floss was terribly envious.

It turned out that the woman was in the Voluntary Aid Detachment, the VADs; and she was definitely *not* of the likes of the Loveless family. Beatrice Norton was a wealthy Dorset doctor's daughter 'doing her bit'.

'I'm a trifle cack-handed at this sort of thing,' she explained apologetically. 'You see, when one was growing up, one never had to light a fire, cook a meal, or sweep a floor. One had lots of servants to do the menial tasks. Until I was eighteen I lived most of my life in the schoolroom upstairs where one had one's lessons. One sewed, did embroidery, had tea parties, paid calls, taught at Sunday School, organized bazaars and fêtes, that sort of palaver. Other than that, one never met anyone and one was awfully shy.'

Poor Beatrice had got engaged to a dashing officer in the Dorset Hussars who'd 'dashed off to war and got dashed well killed, poor darling. Dashed bad luck'.

For a moment, her stiff upper lip began to tremble, the posh façade cracked and she murmured, half to herself, 'No one knows how much it takes to serve one's country when all one's loved ones are gone.'

In Beatrice's case: first her fiancé, then her best friend, lastly, her beloved only brother. The sole salvation was to bury herself in work, the tougher and dirtier the better, patching up and repairing the living. It never occurred to her to expect payment.

The two 'scrubbers' may have had little in common, but two things they shared: a hatred of war and an interest in Sylvia Pankhurst's Suffragettes.

'I don't know how one can work in munitions, old thing,' Beatrice remarked matter-of-factly one Sunday. 'Goes against the grain, Florence.'

Floss shrugged. 'How many girls like me have you met in VAD?' she asked.

Beatrice screwed up her eyes and pursed her lips slowly. She said, 'None, come to think of it. We're pretty much a snooty bunch. No hoi-polloi here, old bean. Point taken.'

She gave a guilty smile.

'I'd love to give it up and become a VAD nurse,' said Floss. 'But there's not much chance of that, is there?'

Beatrice's eyes twinkled.

'We sisters must stick together. I'll see what I can do. Must get you out of weaponry.'

Next Sunday, a crafty smile played at the corners of Beatrice's thin lips.

'Right, I've had a word in Matron's ear; she's an old flame of Daddy's. You go before the Board next Wednesday.'

Floss couldn't wait for Wednesday to come round. What was she to tell Harriet H? 'Please, ma'am, I've got an interview for nursing.' In the end, she said nothing, except to Mum and Doss; and she took the day off.

Beatrice had primed her for the Board.

'You are nineteen. You've nursed sick kids. You have your First Aid and Home Nursing certificates, joined the St John's Ambulance Brigade and helped out with the Red Cross. They won't check. And another thing: take Matron a bunch of flowers—I'll bring some crocuses and snowdrops from our garden. Chin up, old girl. Remember: *you* are as good as any of them.'

All the same, when Floss entered the interview room she was quaking in her boots.

'Take a seat, Miss Loveless,' said Matron with a reassuring smile (grateful for the posy). The other seven Board members, six of them men, were not so welcoming. The first question, from a stony-faced, bald-headed man, made her blush.

'What age are you?'

'Nineteen,' she mumbled.

'Speak up, girl. What year were you born?'

Lucky she was quick at mental arithmetic.

'Eighteen ninety seven.'

She could see they didn't believe her.

She told them of her certificates and experience. They quizzed her, dug deeper. Why did she want to nurse? What would she do if . . . ?

After a while she began to resent the questioning. Nursing was something she'd set her heart on. She *knew* she was tough, sensible, and learned quickly. *They* needed nurses. *She* wanted to nurse.

'What does your father think of all this?'

That touched a raw nerve.

'I haven't been able to contact my father. He's in Palestine, you see,' she said tartly; 'and he's gone missing. My *mother* is fully behind me.'

That was one in the eye for old misery-guts.

They took a vote in front of her: four for, four against. The house surgeon was one of the waverers.

'I'm not convinced she has what it takes,' he summed up, as if she wasn't there. 'She'll have to be tested. Arrange it, will you, Matron.'

No 'Dismiss'; no 'Thanks for coming'; no 'No', 'Yes', or 'Maybe'. So what test would it be? Maths? English? Cooking? She was soon to find out.

'Mr Parker-Smythe will be operating after lunch,' said Matron loudly. 'Be in the theatre at two thirty.' Then, in a whisper, she said, 'He wants to test your nerve, thinks you'll keel over at the first sight of blood. Hold up, Florence. Don't let *us* down.'

Floss liked the 'us'. For the first time she felt part of a women's team fighting for something worthwhile. The 'team' stood above where you lived, how you talked, what you did for a living. She was determined not to let *her* team down.

Dead on two thirty, dressed in baggy grey smock, net cap, and white mask, she stood at the operating table. She was already feeling queasy at the sickly-sweet smell of ether mixed with carbolic. A patient—evidently a wounded soldier—lay on the table, knocked out by gas.

In her wildest nightmares, she could never have imagined what was to follow.

'Hold on to the left foot, nurse,' muttered the surgeon through his mask.

The word 'nurse' was music to her ears, and she gladly held the man's leg just below the knee; the top part was covered with sterile towels.

But her pleasure quickly turned to terror as the surgeon made an incision, picked up a saw, and set to cutting through skin and bone. He was amputating the leg!

She all but threw up there and then; she suddenly saw two legs and two saws dancing before her eyes. It was lucky she was holding on to something—the gammy leg.

Now or never. 'Hold up!' Matron had urged. It was hold up or throw up! But hold up she would. She knew that if she saw the blood gushing out, she'd be done for. So, desperately looking towards the far wall, she filled her mind with other images: squashed tomatoes for bloody flesh; boiled cabbage smells for rotting tissue; 'stemming' shells for cracking bones.

Think of the poor soldier with one leg.

Think of apple cores, snotty noses, daisies, tadpoles, jamjars, bluebottles—anything but a sawn-off limb. She recited a popular ditty, over and over again:

> 'Take me back to dear old Blighty,
> Put me on the train for London town.
> Take me over there,
> Drop me anywhere . . . '

Just when she thought the ordeal was over, the surgeon casually remarked, 'Put the stump in the bucket, will you, nurse, and take it to the incinerator. Then report to my office.'

With that he washed his hands and went out, leaving her alone.

She stared at the one-legged man lying on the table—and the sawn-off leg beside him. The leg looked so alive, bleeding from the arteries, its pink tissue quivering like a stranded fish.

Somehow she had to get the leg from table to bucket without touching it! She picked up the white slop bucket, already full of bloody swabs, and set it beneath the leg; then with a mop handle she pushed the leg towards the edge of the table, trying to tip it into the pail.

It wasn't going to work. Blood spilled over the green lino as the leg poked out like a yardarm. There was nothing for it. Taking a deep breath, she picked up the still warm limb in both hands and dropped it—plop!—into the bucket.

Handling a squirming snake could not have been more terrifying. Even when she grasped the metal pail handle, the leg rocked to and fro against her hand as she hurried down the corridor, out of the door, and across the yard to the incinerator.

Luckily for her, old 'Smokin' Joe', the incinerator man, was still on duty.

'Ah, a nice roast drumstick for me supper,' he said gaily. 'Ta, gal.'

She dropped the bucket and ran.

At the back of the yard was a gate which she quickly opened and passed through into Pitt Street beyond. She leaned against the fence and watched the passers-by, people who knew nothing of the burning bits of flesh a few feet from them.

After a few minutes, her lungs cleansed with fresh air, she forced her mind back to the hospital.

'There's only one question to answer,' she told herself sternly. 'Do you want to help the sick and wounded or not? If you do, get back in and report to the sawbones.'

In his office Mr Parker-Smythe asked grumpily, 'Well, do you still want to be a nurse?'

'Yes, I do.' Her voice echoed loudly round the room.

'There's no need to shout,' he muttered. 'Jolly good. But God help you!'

7

They would not have us weep . . .
  Dear boys of ours, whom we have lost awhile;
Rather they'd have us keep
  Brave looks, and lips that tremble to a smile.
They would not have us grieve—
  Dear boys of ours, whose valiant hearts are stilled;
Nor would they have us leave
  OUR task undone, OUR service unfulfilled.

Helen Sevrez

For the first time in their lives the twins went their separate ways. Floss handed in her notice at the dockyard—only a fortnight after starting work. Although Mrs Ha-Ha fussed and fumed, the covering note from Matron settled it.

'Namby-pamby nurses aren't proper war workers in my book,' she growled. 'That's a job for lily-handed ladies who know no better, see. No pay in it either. At least your sister cares about her family . . . Mark my words, Miss Florence, you'll be on your knees begging for your job back before the month is out!'

'I *won't* be back,' was all Floss said.

But the dragon woman had touched a raw nerve. Mum being Mum was right behind her in the nursing career. But Doss said what Mum was probably thinking—in her usual blunt way.

'It's your life, sis. But you're letting Mum and the kids down. My three quid won't go far. At a time like this too . . .'

The 'time like this' involved news of Dad. For the moment Floss felt that, apart from Mum, the whole world was against her—her own sister, dockyard workmates, the Lady Welfare Supervisor, even the hospital staff she was to work with. One lot thought her too snooty, the other lot too common.

Still, Doss was right about one thing. Mum really did need all the support she could get.

When the twins came home from work at seven on Tuesday evening, there was no tea on the table, the kids were howling, and Mum was sitting in the chair, head in hands. She was staring dumbly at a printed piece of paper.

She didn't say a word in answer to their 'What's up, Mum?' But they guessed. The only question was: which one, Jack or Dad?

Floss hurriedly picked up the letter, damp and smudged from Mum's tears.

It was a standard letter, marked B 104 83, from the Army Record Office. The tone was stiff and formal. Dad's details had been penned in the gaps:

Sirs,

I regret to have to inform you that a report has been received from the War Office to the effect that

(No.)	*233873 (9147)*
(Rank)	*Private*
(Name)	*Bertram Frank Loveless*
(Regiment)	*15th Hampshire*

was posted as missing in the Field
(on the) *16th Day of December 1916*

43

I am, Sir,
Your obedient servant

J. V. S. Gunn

Officer in charge of Records

There was a hush, even from the kids, then a loud sigh of relief from Doss.

'Oh, is that all? He's only missing, Mum. Dad'll turn up, you'll see. Most likely lost his way in a sandstorm, bumped into an Egyptian mummy.'

Doss's attempt at cheering her up fell on deaf ears.

'I just knew that'd happen once you started work,' she muttered.

The twins exchanged glances: was Mum going off her rocker?

'But, Mum,' said Floss gently, 'all it says is that Dad went missing on 16th December; we were helping out at school then, remember?'

'Why's it taken six weeks to let us know?'

'Well, maybe they waited for him to show up? You know, not wanting to put the wind up us.'

'Best leave her be,' whispered Floss to her sister. 'Let's make her a nice cup of Rosie Lee. Three sugars. Settle her nerves.'

Tired as they were, the twins set about the unfinished chores: they tidied up, got the tea, made the fire, changed Joey's nappies, fed the little 'uns on bread and tinned milk, gave them all a bath and tucked them into bed.

As sod's law would have it, a second letter had come the same day—from Jack. It lay unopened on the sideboard. Floss tore it open and read out Jack's news.

He'd killed a million more lice than Germans. He had a near miss from a grenade that landed beside him—quick as a flash, he picked it up and lobbed it back, like a cricket ball to the bowler. He'd shared Floss's cake with his mates—now they all wanted to write to his kid sister.

How were his rabbits? The nippers? Pompey? The twins' jobs?

And so he went on. Mum seemed not to hear.

So the twins sat round the fire with her, trying to take her mind off the war by prattling on about the 'cards' at work—'Dotty Bea at the hospital'; 'Vulture Harriet of Workshop No. 5'.

Slowly they eased her out of her stupor. The hot tea helped: it trickled down to revive the dead senses, warmed up her spirit until she began to nod and smile wanly.

At around nine o'clock they led her upstairs to bed. They'd already popped the stone hot-water bottle between the sheets. While Doss sat at her bedside until she nodded off, Floss nipped next door to Mrs Jones for a quiet word.

When the twins left home for work next day, the neighbour dropped in as if on the off-chance, making sure Mum didn't do anything silly.

A third letter arrived a week later. Again it was a long buff envelope with OHMS—On His Majesty's Service—in the top left-hand corner.

It could only mean one of three things: dead, wounded, or taken prisoner. Bad news anyway. Pray God it wasn't the first.

It lay there on the table when Floss came home. Doss wasn't in yet. Joey was asleep, and most of the kids were flicking fag cards at the wall.

'The postman brought it at lunchtime,' Mum said in a wobbly voice. 'I was waiting for you to come home.'

Poor Mum was trembling and ashen-faced.

As Floss picked up the letter she saw at once it had an Aldershot postmark. Was that a hopeful sign?

'Right, Mum,' she said, taking charge. 'I'll first make a cup of tea; then we'll read it together.'

A few minutes later, as they sat side by side at the kitchen table, Floss slit open the letter and pulled out the single sheet of paper. The message was short, the news totally unexpected. She scanned the words a few times before saying breathlessly, 'It's all right, Mum. Dad's *safe*. He's back home in England, a bit sick—doesn't say what with—in Aldershot's Cambridge Hospital.'

She suddenly looked up in surprise.

'Well, I'm darned, that's where I'm going on training next week.'

'Does it say we can see him?' asked Mum.

'No, but I'll soon find out.'

Floss thought she'd better make enquiries; it wouldn't do for Mum to see a half-mangled, legless wreck.

Just then, Dossie breezed in.

'I'm off out, there's a dance at the pier,' she cried, rushing to the kitchen sink to wash. 'Do us a slice of bread and dripping, Floss.'

Mum's words stopped her in her tracks.

'Dad's home . . .'

'What? Where? How?'

'In hospital, Aldershot,' explained her sister. 'We don't know *how* he is; I'll try to find out.'

'See, I said he'd be fine. Good old Dad.'

They could hear splashing and snatches of song from the kitchen sink:

'Who were you with last night,
Out in the pale moonlight?
It wasn't your brother, it wasn't your pa,
Ah, ah, ah, ah, ah-ha, ah-ha.

'Hey, Flo, why don't we cycle up to Aldershot on Sunday? Mum could go on the train. Mrs Jones'll look after the kids. Did you see that Zeppelin come over today? They say it was taking photos of places for Jerry to land, cheeky beggars. I can't get the hang of this new make-up, I'm always smudging the lipstick.'

Mum was infected by Doss's high spirits.

'Perhaps I'd better powder my nose, rouge my cheeks, and paint my lips for your dad,' she said with a smile.

It was the first time she'd smiled in a week.

8

'Valueless, A Duffer!' says the Sister's face,
When I try to do her orders with my bestest grace.
'Vain And Disappointing!' says Staff Nurse's eye,
If I dare to put my cap straight while she's walking by.

'Very Active Danger', looks the angry pro.,
If I sometimes score a wee bit over her, you know.
'Virtuous And Dumpty!' that's the way I feel,
When I'm uniformed from cap strings to each wardroom
*   heel.*
'Vague And Disillusioned' that's my mood each night,
When I've tried all day to please 'em and done nothing
*   right.*

'Valiant And Determined', I arise next day,
As I tell myself it's <u>duty</u> and I must obey.
'Very Anxious Daily' I await my leave,
Which I spend with my <u>own</u> soldier, as you may believe.
'Verily A Darling' that's his name for me.
When I meet him in my uniform of V A D.

Written by a VAD's mother

If Floss thought being a VAD meant tending sick soldiers, she was soon proved wrong. Being a trainee, she was at the beck and call of every Tom, Dick, and Harry—or, in her case, Matron, Sister, and Staff Nurse. She got the dirtiest, battiest, grisliest of jobs.

Most of her time was spent doing the washing up. Mountains and mountains of it. As soon as she finished one lot, it was time to set the trays for another meal, and in half an hour she had to start washing up in cold water all over again.

The wards had bare wooden floors and every morning, after breakfast, she had to take all the tea leaves from the kitchen and scatter them over the floors to lay the dust and then sweep them up again. Then she had to clean and polish, dust and scrub, wash and disinfect.

The ward routine was very strict, along army lines. It was the VAD's job to see that all the beds were in line, like ranks of guardsmen. Sister would march in, take out her handkerchief to measure the gap between wall and bed, and ensure all the bed castors pointed the same way, not higgledy-piggledy.

The ward was Sister's parade ground, and she ruled it like a sergeant-major.

Then there was medicine. Floss had to learn to give it properly. You didn't just lift a bottle, pour it out, and spoon it in. No, it had to be done by numbers:

'Lift the bottle, two, three, four. Have the label in the palm, and forefinger on the cork. Five, six, seven. Read the label, shake the bottle and pour the required dose. Eight, nine, ten.'

It was the same with bandaging, so many rules, you had to know them all: separate rules for leg wounds, arm wounds, neck wounds, head wounds, back wounds . . .

Men joked they had to die by numbers: 'Close your eyes, two, three, four. Let your mouth fall open, six, seven, eight. One last groan and . . . Wait for it! Wait for it!— Pass away.'

What a palaver! Did it help the men get better or make them feel more comfortable? Of course not. It had always been done this way. But the war and the new nurses were going to change things.

Floss didn't mind too much because that was what

she was there for—taking the humdrum chores off the shoulders of the trained nurses, so they could give all their time to the wounded. Far from being grateful, though, most nurses were resentful of the VADs and treated them like scullery maids.

Now and then it had its lighter side.

One day, the ward duty nurse, Sister Treasure, bumped into Floss and Beatrice in the hospital entrance hall.

'Nurse Norton,' she said sharply, ignoring Floss altogether, 'I want you to take these clean sheets upstairs right away.'

She handed Bea a huge armful of starched sheets before departing up the main staircase.

Naturally, Bea followed her up the stairs, holding the pile of sheets in her arms. When she was halfway up, Sister Treasure leaned over the top banister and called down in a loud voice, 'Nurse Norton! Where on earth do you think you're going? VADs use the back stairs!'

As she came back down the stairs, Beatrice had a wry smile on her face. Floss only saw the funny side when the doctor's daughter explained.

'Oh my, Florence, it's hard to be humble when you've known people in another life, before *all this*.'

'Do you *know* Sister Treasure then?'

'Oh yes, she used to be our parlourmaid . . .'

War certainly had upset the apple-cart, put the boot on the other foot. But they both had a good titter, especially Beatrice.

Floss came to grow fond of her companion. Though they'd been born and bred worlds apart, neither skimped on effort or let the other down. That brought them together.

One time, Beatrice exclaimed, holding up her hands, 'When I wanted to take up nursing, my mother warned, "But, darling, it will ruin your hands!" Now, look at them.'

Her once-soft, manicured hands were red, raw, and rough, chiefly from the carbolic acid they used for disinfectant.

Floss couldn't help admiring her. She was always rushing here and there, her feet swelling up through the laces of her worn flat-soled shoes; she emptied the bedpans with scarcely a wrinkle of her dainty nose; she held kidney trays, looking on while doctors probed and dressed wounds so terrible that only the most hardened of stomachs could bear the sight. Despite all that, doctors, and particularly the trained nurses, rarely treated her with good grace.

On her evenings off, she would whisk Floss off to the local pub. What a transformation. She did things Floss had never dared do. To say she let her hair down meant she put her hair *up*—and wore trousers, smoked from a cigarette holder, flattened her chest to look like a man and, worst of all, she ordered a whole pint of beer.

It scared the pub regulars and sometimes made Floss blush. Yet she enjoyed the seeds of doubt sown in male minds.

Back on duty, the bedridden soldiers had their own names for VADs like Bea and Floss. In Bea's case, it was Very Awkward Duffer; in Floss's it was Very Active Duster. At worst, they were 'Victim Always Dies'. That was the men's standing joke.

That wasn't all. When soldiers were in great pain, they often turned the air blue with curses that Bea, with her sheltered upbringing, had never heard in her life. She relied on Floss to tell her what they meant!

While they were on their knees scrubbing the ward floor, Floss told Beatrice about Dad.

'He's back home, being seen to at the Cambridge in Aldershot.'

'For special head cases,' was all Beatrice said.

Floss was taken aback by the clipped tone. As she glanced sideways she noticed a puckering of the brow and pursed lips.

'We're planning a family visit on Sunday, the whole tribe,' continued Floss. 'Funny that, I start my training there on Monday.'

The information was met in silence.

'Did *you* train there?'

'No.'

They rinsed the floorcloths and soaped the scrubbing brushes before carrying on without a word. Beatrice was too much of a chatterbox to keep up the silence for long.

'Look, old bean, it's none of my business. But I wouldn't take the family over just yet. Best to see the way the land lies, don't you know.'

'What do you mean?'

'It's a bit hush-hush, old fruit. But since you'll be training there, you'll find out anyway. Pater does a spot of consulting at the Cambridge. You see . . . the poor blighters aren't so much sick in body, more in the mind, so to speak.'

She wouldn't say more, but it was clear she was concerned for Floss's sake.

Floss didn't know what to make of it. She'd heard of soldiers going goofy; but surely they soon came out of it, like from a giddy spell. All the same, she took Beatrice's advice and warned off her family.

'Dad's not allowed visitors till he's on the mend. I'll tell you what I can next week.'

She took the train for Aldershot early Monday morning, and was met at the hospital by Matron, a small, busy, middle-aged woman who had to crane her neck to look at the new girl. What she lacked in inches, however, she made up for in fierceness.

She looked Floss up and down as if she was a

52

music hall chorus girl. What she saw obviously displeased her.

'Why's your hair like a mophead?'

Matron's eyes swept all the way down to the feet.

'Only shameless hussies show naked ankles for men to ogle.'

Floss would like to have told her that short skirts were patriotic—answering the country's call for saving on cloth which was sorely needed for uniforms and blankets. But she bit her tongue. If she wanted to qualify, she had to keep mum, bow her head, and stand to attention.

'Go and cover yourself up, girl.'

Floss was directed to the clothing stores where she was soon kitted out. Her hopes of pulling on a smart uniform like Beatrice's were swiftly dashed. Queen Victoria herself would not have raised an eyebrow at the picture presented by Trainee Florence Loveless.

The uniform consisted of a long black cloak over a grey dress with little braid-edged shoulder cape, a small black bonnet made of straw and trimmed with a black velvet bow secured to her head by narrow white strings. The cloak came to within an inch of the ground and hid most of the thick black woollen stockings she had to wear.

Dressed in these drab 'passion killers', Floss reported back to Matron. Her scrubbing and washing up skills were evidently taken as read; here she was solely to help out with medical duties on the wards.

'A word of warning to you, Nurse Loveless,' snapped Matron. 'Most of the patients here are, well, let's say a bit unhinged. Night-time's the worst.'

Wondering at these words, Floss made her way through the hospital grounds to what Matron had called her 'billet'. Her training was to last three weeks, with day and night shifts, so she'd be sleeping in the nurses' dormitory, beside the hospital.

The inside of the hospital was light and airy, with white or pea-green walls, a pleasant change from the gloomy dark brown of the Royal. And since it was out of town, the place was very peaceful, surrounded by rolling countryside. Floss looked forward to her stay here; it was the first time in her life she'd lived away from home and town.

Although it was still winter, men were dotted about the grounds, some sitting in wheelchairs, their legs covered by warm rugs; some were lounging on chairs beneath trees, some were strolling about, heads gravely bowed; some merry souls were chattering away to themselves.

On her way to the dormitory, Floss searched the haggard, strangely wild faces for her father. And, all at once, she saw him, all alone against a wall. He was sitting in a wheelchair, staring fixedly at the grass before him.

'Dad, Dad,' she cried, running towards him.

He glanced up at her happy, smiling face. But his features showed no sign of recognition. He just stared straight through her.

'It's me, Dad—Florence. I'm a nurse.'

The word 'nurse' seemed to rouse him. He tried to form a word; but all that came out was white foam dribbling down his chin. She quickly wiped it away with her sleeve, put her arms round him in a warm hug . . . and wept.

9

When the Vision dies in the dust of the market place,
When the Light is dim,
When you lift up your eyes and cannot behold his face,
When your heart is far from him,

Know this is your War; in this lonely hour you ride
Down the roads he knew;
Though he comes no more at night he will kneel at
   your side
For comfort to dream with you.
'When the Vision Dies' by May Wedderburn Cannan

Floss had spent no more than a few minutes with her father before a male orderly came up to wheel him inside. He was a cheery nuggety sort of man with an ugly hump on his back.

'Hello, ducks,' he said in greeting. 'You won't get a peep out of old Bertie. Tighter than a camel's proverbial in a sandstorm.'

He clearly had no idea she was his daughter; and Floss wasn't going to put him wise.

'What's the matter with him?' she asked innocently.

'Oh, the usual. They've different names for it. I calls it shell-shock; war's shaken their brains up, poor blighters. In the army's book, though, they're either off their rocker or putting it on to avoid fighting. Can't have them undermining the war effort now, can we?'

'What happened to this poor man?'

'Bert? I heard he chucked away his gun and went walkies in the desert. They picked him up a few days later suffering from sunstroke, collywobbles, you-name-it-he-had-it. I guess he just didn't wanna fight no more. That's about the size of it.'

'Will he get better?'

'Might be better if he didn't, poor sod. He could stay loopy for the rest of his natural, seeing sights we're lucky not seeing. On the other hand, *if* he recovers, he's likely to face the music for deserting his post.'

'Then what?'

'Oh, they'll shoot him.'

Floss's hand flew to her mouth as the picture of Nurse Cavell's last moments came to mind. But she had faced a *German* firing squad! How could the British shoot their own, someone who didn't know what he was doing?

'If you wanna know more about him, ask his mate; he was with him in Gyppoland. Over there—the poor legless bleeder in the wheelchair.'

Floss glanced over to a figure beneath an apple tree and committed his face to memory. If she didn't make herself short right now, Matron'd have her guts for garters.

'Er, thanks . . . Mr?'

'Eric, miss. Eric Burman.'

'Cheerio, Eric.'

'Good-bye-ee! Don't cry-ee! There's a sil-ver lining in the sky-ee, Bon-soir, old thing! cheer-i-o! chin-chin. Nah-poo! Too-dle-oo! Good-bye-ee!' sang Eric as he wheeled the patient back to the hospital.

Floss trudged off in the opposite direction with thoughts of Dad troubling her. What was she to tell Mum . . . and Doss? Maybe Dad'd make a speedy recovery? But the quicker he got better, the closer he came to the firing squad. Death by memories or death by shooting. Not a pleasant choice. Poor Dad. Poor Mum.

At the nurses' quarters, the housekeeper soon found her a billet in the long dormitory. At least it was a bed to herself, not like at home where she shared a bed, two up, two down, and always had the kids' cheesy feet in her nose and mouth.

She unpacked her bag, put her flannel nightie under the pillow, and her wash things in the bedside drawer. Then she hurried back to Matron.

'Ah, that's more like it,' declared Matron, looking her up and down. 'There's more of the nurse than the tart about you now. You can't beat an old-fashioned nurse's uniform for smartness.'

Floss stood to attention before her, head dutifully bent, mouthing 'Yes, Matron. Thank you, Matron.' Suddenly the little old shrew looked at her watch and frowned.

'Look here, I have to do the rounds. Go and familiarize yourself with the wards and case histories—so's you know what we're dealing with here. Oh, and take this hospital magazine. Doctor Roberts thinks it good for the men. It'll give you an insight into their sick minds. Be back spot on midday.'

That gave Floss an hour to wander round. The hospital was a melancholy place, not unpleasant to the eye; it was the human debris inside it that gave it a sad, gloomy air.

Men with dulled, sunken eyes, haggard, hopeless faces, hunched shoulders, like Atlas carrying the world's woes upon his back.

She made her way through wards lined with twenty beds on each side. At the end of one ward were some french doors leading into the gardens. She was glad to get a breath of February's bracing air.

Dad and his legless mate were nowhere to be seen.

Cheery Eric had told her they were due for therapy in the gym.

She sat on a wooden bench to leaf through the hospital magazine. *The Hydra*. It contained a mixture of poems and personal accounts of men's nightmares.

These were cries of pain from soldiers battle-tested till they cracked. Most painful of all was what one patient saw in his dreams each night:

'Wounded German soldiers are lying on the ground, and our tanks are bearing down on them. They raise their arms, pleading to be spared. But the tanks come on and on, and mow them down. Oh, the terrible screams haunt me still, the sight of blood and flesh squeezed out of the tank tracks, the crunching of bones and skulls. Help me!'

Another wrote of seeing a trenchful of about a hundred soldiers, waiting for the order to go 'over the top'. All at once, a shell burst among them, making their trench tumble in and burying them alive.

'Night after night I see their bayonets and guns sticking out of the earth.'

A voice behind her made her jump.

'You're Bert's gal, ain't yuh?'

As she whipped round, she was astonished to see the wheelchair-bound soldier pointed out to her as Dad's mate.

'But which one, eh? Florence or Dorothy? Mmmm, I'd plump for Florence.'

'How on earth did you know that?' she exclaimed, as he wheeled himself round to the front of the bench.

'Blimey, I'd recognize you anywhere. Your dad hardly talked of anything else out in Palestine. Anyway, I saw you fussing over him earlier. Nurses don't blubber over patients. But gals do over dads.'

'Is he always like that?' she asked.

'Most of the time. He comes to life at night, though, throws a paddy, fights anyone in sight as if he's back in the war.'

'Will they really shoot him when he's better?'

'Now who's been blabbin'? Our Hunchback of Notre Dame, I betcha. Well, bluntly, Miss Florence, there's a fair chance. The army brands him a deserter, just because he upped and scarpered. I know better: a braver man than your dad don't walk the earth. But ever since that bleedin' shell went and knocked him out, he started acting queer. In the end, he just couldn't take it any more and tried to get hisself killed.'

'Poor Dad,' sighed Floss.

'Knowing your old man, he'll do anything to cheat the beggars, even if it means croakin'. Beg pardon, Miss Florence.'

'Not if I can help it!' she said defiantly. 'I'll get him better and take on the whole army if I have to. I'll show them Dad can't answer for his actions.'

'Good for you, gal,' he said with a grin, wheeling himself about.

He trundled off, muttering and shaking his head. She caught the words, 'Right chip off the old block . . . '

10

Earning high wages? Yus,
  Five quid a week.
A woman, too, mind you,
  I calls it dim sweet.

Ye' are asking some questions—
  But bless yer, here goes:
I spends the whole racket
  On good times and clothes.

*   *   *

Worthwhile, for tomorrow
  If I'm blown to the sky,
I'll have repaid mi wages
  In death—and pass by.
  from 'Munition Wages' by Madeleine Ida Bedford

In the meantime, Doss was enjoying the new freedom her munitions job earned her. There was so much she could do that girls had been denied before. And although she was surrounded on all sides by busybodies 'concerned' for her welfare, morals, and safety, Doss made her own choices with her own sort.

So, while the YWCA thumped the tub for God's games, like netball, hockey, and tennis, Doss had her own ideas about how to spend her free time. Mind you, she was up against the world expert on women's games—Mrs Ha-Ha. One lunchtime, she gave one of her regular lectures in the canteen: on 'Women's Recreation'.

'You women workers must take healthy exercise, get out into the fresh air, re-create your energies for work. A healthy mind in a healthy body!

'But you should know what is good for you and what not. Swimming, gymnastics, netball, cricket, hockey—all jolly good fun and healthy recreation. The dockyard has formed clubs for you, and made baths, halls, and sports fields available free.

'However, some sports are harmful to a woman's organism. I refer especially to football; this is definitely *not* a suitable game for girls. It is played by rough types, it's most unladylike, and it can cause serious injuries to your child-bearing apparatus. After all, that *is* your main function in life: having children.

'Worst of all, bare legs and wobbly chests can cause unhealthy excitement among males. I tremble to think what that might lead to. You are *not*, I repeat NOT, to play football or suchlike coarse pursuits.'

Naturally, Doss and her workmates went right out and played football. That was one in the eye for fuddy-duddies like Ha-Ha and her YWCA blue stockings. It was a daring choice, for women hadn't played the game before the war. Doss herself formed a works team called 'The Canaries' which issued challenges to other workshops and factories around town.

Even though they had to dodge women's patrols, policewomen, and YMCA workers who tried to break up the games, women's teams soon sprang up and played their matches on common land.

Since she couldn't stop it, Mrs Ha-Ha detailed a nurse to accompany the works football team, and had policewomen patrol the 'rough, riotous matches'. To her football was just one example of base habits and revolt among women who no longer knew their place. Roll on the war's end and restoration of order and decency.

61

Another sport Doss enjoyed was cycling. With her first month's wages, she had rescued Jack's bike and Mum's wedding ring from the pawnshop. And of a Sunday, when she wasn't running the football team, she'd cycle off with her girlfriends and their younger brothers for a day-long outing.

Most of them had joined the Clarion Cycling Club which they regarded as their own; it didn't preach religion or prattle on about bare legs or bathing costumes. Doss and her mates would cycle to the New Forest, paddle in streams, have a picnic, sing and play, and finish off with a shandy in a country pub.

To many girls like Doss, war had changed their world beyond recognition. They were seeing their actual or future mates swept away by that ever-growing tidal wave of war. How could you believe in religion when men were being carved up and murdered in their millions by Christian nations?

It is hardly surprising that many young women lived and loved for the moment. The old ideals of how a woman should behave were fast disappearing forever in the turmoil of war. So they grabbed what they could, while they could. 'Live, laugh, love, and be happy—for tomorrow you may die' was their motto.

Every day at work Doss saw how thin the line was between life and death. More than one woman had got her hair caught in machinery and lost part of her scalp. Some women had lost fingers or a hand in the moving parts, and they all *knew* they were being poisoned, slowly but surely, by TNT.

They could feel it inside them; they could see it in the yellow of their hands and faces, in their ginger hair. Everything they touched turned to 'gold'—chairs, tables, clothes. Not only that, many came out in rashes, their faces swelled up, and some even went blind.

Although in the trams the 'canaries' kept men at bay, scared of being infected by these ghastly women, the 'yellow fever' also frightened off boyfriends too. Doctors, of course, assured them it was harmless and temporary. But the newspapers told a different story, regularly reporting on women dying of TNT poisoning.

When a girl called Florence Gleave died, the *Daily Chronicle* proudly headlined her dying words to her father: 'If I die, they can only say I've done my bit.'

Doss had already seen a shell blow up in her best friend's face—poor May lost her pretty blue eyes and half her snub nose. How life hung by a thread really came home to her one night when she'd just started her night shift.

The workshop next door cooked cordite paste in a big stove. When it was baked hard into long cords, it was packed into shells and other explosive devices. One night, someone was putting a load of raw cordite into the stove when there was a Godalmighty explosion.

Next thing Doss knew a blast of air shot her head first out of the workshop door, down the steps and into the ice-cold gooey mud of the yard.

As she was lying there, numb with shock, she heard more big bangs, and she watched as in a dream while a huge mushroom spiral of smoke, sparks, and debris rose into the sky. Bodies were flying through the air over the workshop roof. For some stupid reason, they reminded her of Peter Pan and the Darling children flying to Never-Never Land.

For one awful moment Doss thought that perhaps she was already dead. But after pinching herself, she found that, apart from singed hair, cuts and bruises, she was still in one piece. She pulled herself up and began to wipe the mud from eyes and ears.

It had all happened in a split second, yet already

crowds were rushing towards the two crumbling workshops. Still dazed, she gazed in horror as they carried out men and women with practically all their clothes burned off, their faces black and charred, some bleeding from holes where limbs had once been, some whose eyes and hair had gone up in smoke.

In no time at all, carts, lorries, and ambulances were carrying their gruesome loads to hospital. Doss herself was stretchered off, suffering from shock, cuts, and bruises.

She learned afterwards that sixty-nine had been killed and over four hundred injured—at least, those were the official figures; some reckoned the real numbers were much higher.

Amid the horror of it all, Doss's main thought was of Floss's face when she saw her sister being wheeled in. And she'd tell Floss, 'Now you know what you're missing in munitions!'

11

The pain and laughter of the day are done,
So strangely hushed and still the long ward seems,
Only the Sister's candle softly beams.
Clear from the church nearby the clock strikes 'one';
And all are wrapt away in secret sleep and dreams.

Here one cries sudden on a sobbing breath,
Gripped in the clutch of some incarnate fear:
What terror through the darkness draweth near?
What vanished scenes of dread to his closed eyes appear?

Through the wide open window one great star,
Swinging her lamp above the pear tree high,
Looks in upon these dreaming forms that lie
So near in body, yet in soul as far
As those bright worlds thick strewn on that vast depth of
  sky.

from 'Night Duty' by Eva Dobell

Floss heard of the explosion from a nurse. It worried her sick, wondering if Doss was safe. But there was little she could do, Matron was unsympathetic.

'You're in the army now, Nurse Loveless. People are being killed and wounded all the time; that's why you're here. If you want to run home to Mummy, you'll have to do it in your own time.'

Her *own* time?

She was doing night shift, on the go every minute of the long night—twelve hours on the trot. Whereas other

65

hospitals were at their busiest in the daytime, this one came alive at night, when darkness fell and ghosts came out to haunt the wards.

'Alive' wasn't really the word for it, since men lay awake, half dead, listening to phantom feet padding along passages and seeing dead comrades hover above them.

Floss went off duty at six thirty each morning, snatched a bite to eat, then flopped down on her bed and dozed off, fully-clothed: she slept and slept and slept—until the whirling misery-go-round started all over again.

Although she never let on about Dad, she spent as much time with him as she could. She would wipe the sweat from his brow and dribble from his chin, spoon soup and porridge into his mouth, read him Jack's letters. But even she could do nothing about his shaking fits. The tremors would come on all of a sudden. He would sit up in bed, trembling all over, his mouth working at strangled screams that never found a way out. It took two strong orderlies to hold him down while waiting for the Medical Officer to stick a needle in his arm.

The wards were full of men whose slumbers were terrifying, who dreaded falling asleep for fear of what they would see. Each would be back in the trenches, reliving the horrors that had tipped them over the edge into the black abyss.

She felt so helpless—but no more than the rest of the medical staff. Nothing had prepared any of them for dealing with shell-shocked soldiers, men who'd seen things they couldn't begin to imagine. How could nurses understand the terrors of the Front?

For Floss, concern for patients was now mixed with worry about her sister. It nagged at her until she too found sleep hard to grasp for more than an hour at a stretch. She knew she just had to steal a few waking hours for a trip home. With any luck, she could snatch forty winks on the train, pop home for a couple of hours, and be back in time for the night shift.

So, two days after the dockyard disaster, she walked the five miles to Aldershot Station, caught the eight o'clock train, changing at Winchester and Southampton, and got in at ten. A friendly coalman gave her a lift on his horse and cart; so she arrived in style, sitting amongst the sacks of coke and coal.

No one in the street had seen a nurse outside hospital before, least of all one on a coal cart. She gave the family quite a shock, marching into the house in her VAD uniform. The kids stared goggle-eyed, as if she was the midwife or beadle. Doss looked up from her makeshift bed on the settee.

'Well, look who it isn't,' she exclaimed with a startled smile; 'the Lady with the Lamp.'

'Oh my,' mumbled Mum unsurely, 'what'll the neighbours think?'

Not 'Oh, Florrie, how lovely to see you. How are you? How's Dad', but 'What'll the neighbours think?' The war hadn't changed Mum.

'Blow the neighbours,' said Floss. 'How are you, sis? Still in one piece, I see.'

She grinned with relief. It was obvious from the bandaged arm and ankle, as well as the few grazes on her face, that she'd survived intact.

'What's the use of having a nurse for a sister if she's not there to patch you up?' muttered Doss.

Floss sank down on a chair and took off her straw bonnet.

'Anyway, what's the news of Dad?' asked Doss.

Floss tried not to let her face betray her. She shook free her hair, looked away, and said brightly, 'Oh, he's coming along fine. He got knocked out by a shell, no harm done to life and limb; he's still dazed though. Dad'll pull through, you know what he's like, tough as old boots.'

Mum suddenly found her voice; it all came gushing out as from an uncorked bottle.

'What does he say? When can we see him? When's he coming home? I gotta air the room, make egg custard, get some things in.'

Floss wasn't prepared for Mum's questions.

'Gi's a break, Mum. I'm all in. How about a cuppa? I've been up all night.'

She needed time to think.

Twenty minutes later, Mum was pouring the last dregs through the strainer, and Floss was on her third cup of tea. Right, now or never; she couldn't put it off any longer. She closed her eyes, blotting out the tense, expectant faces before her, and said slowly, 'Dad's still woozy . . . but he's on the mend. It's likely to take a while before he's himself again. He'll pull through . . . Doctors don't advise visitors yet . . . Er, he may not recognize you, see; he doesn't always know me . . .'

'Why? Has he gone blind?'

'No, Mum. It's just that his mind's a blank, like someone who's lost his memory. 'S only temporary. His body's OK; not a scratch.'

They evidently didn't understand. But Doss wasn't one to beat about the bush.

'He hasn't gone barmy, has he?'

'No, no, no . . .'

Her reply was too hasty to be convincing. But they could see she was done in, and Mum turned her attention from Dad to the weary nurse. She fussed over her, touched her cape gingerly as if it was the Crown Jewels, brushed coal dust from her collar and cuffs.

'Who'd have thought it, my girl a nurse. My, my, my. Pity Gran's not here to see you.'

All at once, she threw up her hands and rose quickly from the chair.

'Come on, love, up the apples and pears. Get some shut-eye. Doss'll help me keep the kids quiet. I'll wake you in an hour, eh? Fancy coming all this way; you shouldn't have bothered. I don't know. I don't know.'

Floss was glad to escape further questions. Mum helped her off with her uniform, took it downstairs and left her in peace.

The moment Floss's head touched the pillow she sank into a sleep so deep no dreams could reach her. All the same, it seemed only minutes later she heard Mum's voice at the foot of the stairs, 'Floss, time to get up. Florence!'

Her sister had limped down to the corner shop and bought a lardy cake and pound of broken toffee. Mum had a jam sandwich ready, and a letter and parcel of clean clothing for Dad. Floss's uniform was neatly laid out, freshly cleaned and ironed, but still damp. She put it on all the same, said her goodbyes to all the family and hurried off to the station.

By five to six she was back in her billet. Twenty-five minutes to go. After no more than a lick and a promise under the basin tap, she examined herself in the cracked mirror, rubbed her dusty shoes with a newspaper, hitched up her black stockings and tugged down her frock. Mum had done a good job of cleaning her uniform.

Every nurse had to appear before matron or duty sister before they went on duty. Today, being Friday, it was Sister Muir in charge. Sister Muir was built like a battleship and now came rocking through choppy waters to inspect the rigid line of duty VADs and nurses. She wasn't in the best of moods.

'Slovenly, the lot of you,' she shouted in a booming voice as she inspected the new shift. 'And another thing: some of you are too familiar with the patients. Treat them well, look after them, but eyes modestly down at all times, and not a peep out of you, remember they have womenfolk of their own.'

Like the others, Floss stood to attention, head bowed, until Sister Muir rolled away, ploughing through the ward and sweeping orderlies out of her way like flapping seagulls.

Floss had several bandaging and cleaning chores before she could snatch a moment for Dad. At last, Mum's precious brown parcel under her arm, she slipped into his ward just before lights out at nine.

All the patients were in bed, except one.

Dad's bed was empty!

12

Light fading where the chimneys cut the sky;
Footsteps that pass,
Nor tarry at my door.
And far away,
Behind the row of crosses, shadows black
Stretch out long arms before the smouldering sun.

*   *   *

But who will give me my children?
from 'The Superfluous Woman' by Vera Brittain

Floss panicked. For the first time in her nursing career.
She stood rooted to the spot, staring down at the neatly
folded-back white sheet on red blanket. Then, as fear gave
way to frenzy, she rushed up and down the ward, hunting
everywhere—bathroom and lavatory, store and staircase.

Finally, all out of breath she ran—smack-bang!—right
into the brick wall of Sister Muir, and bounced off
again.

'What the dickens d'you think you're doing, Miss
Loveless? Get a grip on yourself. I'll not have hysterical
nurses disturbing my patients.'

'He's gone! He's gone!'

Taking Floss firmly by the elbow, the Battleship
whisked her along the corridor and into her office. Once
there, she prodded her into a chair with one finger and
demanded an explanation.

Breathlessly, Floss told her of the empty bed and
missing patient.

'Are you *sure*?' enquired Sister, her voice rising threateningly. 'I checked *myself* just half an hour ago.'

'Dead sure, Sister.'

'Come with me, girl. We'll get to the bottom of this. I'll not have my patients deserting!'

Marching her back down the ward, she stopped at the foot of the unused bed.

'Good God!' was all she said. Then, turning to Floss, she breathed, 'Good work, *nurse*,' stressing the 'nurse'. Sister roughly shook the shoulder of the nearest patient and demanded, 'Where's what's-his-name?'

She read the chartboard clipped to the iron bedstead, 'Private B. Loveless . . . ' Her face slowly changed as the penny dropped. She stared hard at Floss. 'Miss Loveless, are you by any chance related to Private Loveless?'

'He is my father,' came a quivering voice.

'Most irregular,' muttered Sister. 'Poor show. Tut-tut-tut . . . Still, can't be helped; everyone must have a father, I suppose. Got to find the bounder.'

But Dad wasn't to be found. When Sister questioned duty staff, one recalled seeing a fellow in a trench coat over his pyjamas; he was marching across the gardens in his bare feet.

'About sixish, in the dusk,' the man said. 'Odd thing was he had a broom on his shoulder, like doing rifle drill.'

'Couldn't wait to get back to the war,' mumbled Sister, as if she knew about sick-in-the-head patients.

She put a search party together; he *had* to be found. It didn't do to lose patients during her duty shift.

'You go too, Loveless,' she commanded. And in an undertone, she said, 'He's your father, after all. Maybe you can make him see sense. Do your best, girl. Good luck.'

The search party of six fanned out across the grounds: two headed northwards, two east, two west. They calculated that he was unlikely to be going south unless he doubled back towards town. Floss and her old acquaintance Eric Burman took the north-west route.

It had started to rain, a cold slanting drizzle typical of early March. The grass was soft and squelchy underfoot, enough to retain footprints, if there were any. Floss swung the arc of her torch to and fro, looking for any helpful signs. They were almost at the boundary wall when she suddenly spotted the marks of four bare toes in the mud.

'Over here, Mr Burman,' she cried out. 'Looks as if he came this way and scaled the stone wall.'

'If he did,' he muttered, 'he'd have to cross the railway track that runs right by.'

Certainly, someone had leaned a bench against the high wall. It came in handy for Floss to clamber up and over the wall; but her wheezy companion wasn't so agile.

'I can't climb with this monkey on me back,' he said. 'I'll meet you up at the far gate.'

Once over the wall, Floss found herself crunching along the cinders of the main London-to-Winchester railway line. Again her torch caught something in its glow. She gasped. It was a patch of blood caked in mud upon a wooden sleeper.

Poor Dad, she thought, he must've cut his foot on sharp cinders or broken glass.

At least the evidence gave her some bearings. From what she could make out, he was keeping to the railway track instead of wandering off into the woods. She stumbled on beside the far rail, unable to see where she was going in the gloom and rain.

'You've picked a fine night for running away,' she moaned at her father. 'Where on earth do you think you're going?'

Wherever it was, he didn't get far.

As she edged along the mud track by the rail, she trod

on a branch or stick, and heard a loud crack. When she recovered her balance, she saw that it was an old broom; her foot had snapped it in two.

Had he thrown his 'rifle' away again? Marched off into the wilderness? Or would she find him nearby. What crazy thoughts were going through his brain?

It wasn't long before she found the answer to some of those questions.

In the dull grained glare of her torch, she suddenly made out a bundle lying across the tracks—about three yards in front of her. A long object bathed in raindrops lay on one side of the iron rail, and a smaller, round shape, like a football or cabbage, had rolled down the slope on the other side. The torch's pale yellow glow played on it lying in a murky pool.

What on earth was it?

All at once, she realized . . . and let out a sharp cry of terror.

Just at that moment a light was dancing towards her from the opposite direction. Eric's cheery voice rang out, 'Hold on, missie. I'm coming. Watcha got?'

As he came up, she guided his arm towards the bundle.

'It's him, I know it,' she moaned.

She stood as still as the drooping oak trees, turned out her torch, and wept quietly. Her warm tears were quickly chilled by the cleansing rain.

'Oh, my Sainted Aunt!'

The hunchback was bending over the bloodied trench coat and pyjamas.

'Looks like he laid hisself down with the rail as pillow, waiting for the express. Poor bleeder.'

He did his best to comfort the sobbing girl.

'Now, now, missie. Maybe he's better off, poor tortured soul. Did you know him?'

'He was my dad,' she cried through choking sobs.

13

Perhaps some day the sun will shine again,
And I shall see that still the skies are blue,
And feel once more I do not live in vain,
Although bereft of You.

Perhaps some day I shall not shrink in pain
To see the passing of the dying year,
And listen to the Christmas songs again,
Although You cannot hear.

But, though kind Time may many joys renew,
There is one greatest joy I shall not know
Again, because my heart for loss of You
Was broken, long ago.

from 'Perhaps . . . ' by Vera Brittain

They came and gathered up the bits and pieces. These they put into an old potato sack and carried off on a stretcher. It had all to be done in a hurry—before daylight and the next express train.

Floss meanwhile was led back to her billet, dosed with a foul-tasting 'comforter' and put to bed. When she awoke in the morning, her first thought was that it had all been a ghastly dream. But as the light of day filtered into her sleepy head, she saw the stark truth clearly.

Dad had killed himself.

She had to tell Mum and Doss before the army did.

What was she to say?

'Dad had passed away peacefully in his sleep.'

75

'He died a hero.'

Or that he had lain down in his pyjamas, in the rain, upon a railway line and lost his head under an express train's wheels?

If that weren't bad enough, would she tell them something else? Dad would have been shot as a coward if he'd lived. What if the army sent Mum a letter with all the details?

Then another awful truth forced its way into her head. What if they released the body for burial and Mum found two separate pieces?

Her grim musings were interrupted by a visitor. Men weren't allowed into the nurses' quarters. STRICTLY FORBIDDEN! Yet there at the bottom of her bed was a shadowy figure in a wheelchair. That it was a man was obvious from the sour smell of his damp cigarette-smoked clothing.

He held a finger to his lips.

'Shshsh! Don't get the wind up, Miss Florence,' he whispered. 'It's only me, Johnnie Lee, Dad's old mucker.' Seeing her anxiety, he said quietly, 'I slipped by the snoring dragon at the door. I'll be gone in two ticks. I just wanted to give you something.'

He fumbled inside his wet jacket and fished out a crumpled sheet of paper.

'Here, you keep it. Young Lofty gave me it—wrote it hisself, clever old stick. I reckon it sums up yer old man.'

She took it from his hands, modestly pulling the sheets up to her neck.

He gave a toothy smile.

'I told yer he'd cheat them beggars, didn't I? I wish I had his courage. I bet he's up there lookin' down and havin' a good old laugh at 'em.'

'Thank you, Mr Lee,' murmured Floss. 'I'm much obliged.'

His face changed.

'Yeah, well . . . Yer dad was me best mate. You only know what a mate is when ye're under fire. He saved me life—and that of many others. Whatever the army says, it's or'nary soldiers like Bert Loveless who're the real heroes of this bloody war. God rest 'is soul.'

Words broke into sobs and he awkwardly turned himself about, shoulders heaving; he disappeared back the way he'd come.

She sat up in bed, smoothed out the paper and held it up to the window behind her. In dawn's dim light, she read out the verses under her breath.

Young Gunner Jones wasn't keen to go;
He had no quarrel with the foe.
'Your Country Needs You!' people said.
'Do your bit, lad, shoot Germans dead!'

'God be with you,' his mother cried.
In war does God protect one side?
'We're proud of you,' said father to son.
'For King and Country, kill the Hun!'

Bodies, black and broken, covered the muddy ground,
Bombs, shells, and screams crashed all around;
'Kill! Kill! Kill!' bawled Sergeant Dread . . .
He blew his brains out instead . . .

At home no one spoke his name again,
Young Gunner Jones without a brain.
Do those who send our boys to die
Stop to think that war's a lie?

The poem helped make up her mind.
Floss was given two days off. 'Compassionate Leave',

they called it, though Sister Muir was anything but compassionate.

'Go home and grieve. Then forget the moment you get back. Nurses must contain their emotions on duty. They must be hard and stern. If they must cry, they do it on their own, understand?' She changed tack. 'Your father committed a sin in God's sight. But . . . we will say no more about it. Steel yourself against the horrors of war, go home and bury your father's memory.'

Glad of her two days off, Floss kept her mouth tightly shut. She would *never* bury her father's memory; nor had Dad committed any sin in her book.

Instead of going straight home, Floss got off the train at Portsmouth Harbour beside the main dockyard gates. Since she still had her dockyard pass, she slipped by the security police and made her way towards her sister's new Munitions Workshop. It was mid-afternoon and her sister should be 'stemming' away with all the other 'canaries'.

In the outer office, the familiar shape of Mrs Ha-Ha was sitting at her desk. On seeing Floss, a smug look spread over her face.

'Ah, the prodigal daughter returns,' she boomed.

Floss soon soured things.

'I'm here to see my sister. Our dad's dead; I need to break the bad news.'

The 'Vulture' wasn't sympathetic.

'There's a war on. Soldiers die all the time. It's our munitions work that will help bring the boys back home . . .'

Floss wasn't in the mood for sermons.

'Munitions kill,' she said abruptly. 'They killed my father.'

The Welfare Officer's face turned red with anger.

'Your sister finishes her shift in three hours' time, at six thirty precisely. She will not leave a minute early.'

'Right,' said Floss determinedly. 'If you don't let Doss off early I'll take my complaint to the WSPU. We all have a right to compassionate leave for a family loss.'

Mrs Ha-Ha knew all about the Women's Social and Political Union; she well recalled the worktime lost during the rent strike; that was down to them.

'You and your sister are nothing but troublemakers, Suffragist socialists,' she snarled. 'All right, she can go, but she'll have to make up time tomorrow.'

In a fury, she rose from her desk, knocked over the chair and stomped off to fetch Doss. It was obvious from Doss's face as she came through the safety doors that the Vulture had spilled the beans.

The twins walked the three miles home together. It had stopped raining, though the streets were still full of puddles and they had to dodge out of the way of splashes as carts and cars drove by.

Floss had prepared her story.

'Dad died in the night,' she told her sister. 'He wasn't really right in the head after being blown up. Funny thing, he didn't have a scratch on him. Maybe he'd have recovered, maybe not. He didn't suffer any physical pain or anything.'

'Were you with him when he died?'

'No, but I was first on the scene.'

'Where's the funeral? Here or up there?'

She hadn't even given it a thought.

'Dunno. I'll find out.'

You can't lie to your twin. Twins have feelers that reach into each other's brain; they pick up the slightest quiver. It's like one person in two bodies.

Doss knew, but said nothing. Sis must have good reason for keeping quiet; she'd never lie normally. In any case, they had to stand together to prop up Mum.

At the unexpected sight of the two girls coming into

the house, Mum's face went as white as her floury hands.

'Oh no!' she cried. 'It's your dad, I know it. He's gone.'

Wiping her hands on the white apron, she broke down and sobbed uncontrollably. She set off a chain reaction throughout the house. The twins gave in to their feelings and wept; Joey wailed, Reggie moaned, the younger pair of twins blubbered; Timmie, Elsie, and Annie cried their eyes out, not knowing what for.

The entire Loveless household was in mourning.

14

What do you want
Coming to this 'ere 'ell?
Ain't it enough to know he's dead,
Killed by a bit o' German lead?
What!—the Lord means well?

Get out, or I'll strike you down.
I'm carrying his kid.
Do you call that fair?
Gawd—no wonder I wants to gib;
Our first-born, and his father—where?
from 'The Parson's Job' by Madeleine Ida Bedford

Next day a telegram arrived.

No frills this time. No personal message from the King.
No 'We regret to inform you . . . ' Just a brief death notice.

Private Loveless, Bertram, died at the Cambridge
Hospital, Aldershot, on 8 March.
He was buried in Netley Military Cemetery on 9 March.
                    Signed: Captain S. N. Scobey

'What's the rush?' demanded Doss. 'They didn't waste
any time, did they?'

Floss was relieved at the lack of detail.

Mum was upset.

'No chance to say farewell,' she moaned softly. 'They
didn't let me say goodbye to him.'

'Never mind, Mum,' said Floss. 'We can all go and
visit the grave. Next Sunday, eh?'

'At least he's laid to rest in England,' Mum continued, half to herself. 'This blessed war: Dad was against it from the start.'

Floss nodded. Doss shook her head. The kids looked on puzzled.

'The papers are still banging the drum,' exclaimed Floss angrily, 'even though thousands lie dead.'

She had picked up a copy of the *Daily Mail* in the train and now read out one of their patriotic jingles.

> *Who's for the game, the biggest that's played?*
> *The red crashing game of a fight?*
> *Who'll grip and tackle the job unafraid?*
> *And who thinks he'd rather sit tight?*

'Makes you sick, doesn't it?' she continued. 'People like that think war's a game of football played on the green fields of Eton!'

Just then a rat-tat-tat made them jump.

Mum looked up alarmed.

'It can't be old Ebenezer for his rent; it ain't Friday. Don't say it's news of our Jack. Go and see, will you, Dossie.'

Doss returned down the passage with a stranger in black suit and dog collar.

'Heard your bad news, Mrs Loveless,' the stranger said, announcing himself. 'I'm from St Winifred's. Thought I'd come to add a word of comfort.'

He glanced round the room, like a shepherd counting his flock.

'Ta very much, vicar,' said Mum awkwardly. 'Sit yourself down. Would you like a cup of tea?'

'No thanks,' he replied. 'I must soon be on my way. May I say a few words?'

Without waiting for an answer, he pressed on, repeating the same set words he used more and more frequently these days.

'At sad times like this people seek comfort in the Lord. Your husband and father, Bertram, answered his country's call and made the Supreme Sacrifice. Greater love hath no man who giveth his only son. And we are all God's children, are we not?'

He rambled on for a few more minutes before ending with one of his favourite Latin proverbs. He could not have made a graver mistake: *'Dulce et decorum est pro patria mori.'* He smiled sweetly at them all. 'I'll translate for you . . . '

'How sweet and fitting it is to die for one's country.'

The words came from Floss. They surprised the vicar: that such a humble home should know Latin. There was an awkward hush before Mum's voice cut through the silence like a knife.

'Get out!'

Everyone stared at her.

'You come here uninvited, prating on about God, sacrifice, and dying for your country. It's the likes of you who send decent folk like my Bert to his death. How can anyone believe in God when millions are being killed in His name? And all you can do is call for more faith, more sacrifice, more dying . . . I'll tell you what's sweet and fitting: to send you, the army, and the politicians to Hell! Now get out before I kick you out!'

The twins were too taken aback to intervene. They'd never seen Mum like this before.

The vicar grabbed his hat and hastily saw himself out—before this wildcat scratched his eyes out.

Nothing more was said. But the twins added a new respect to the love they had for their mother. War was certainly playing havoc with old ideas.

Next Sunday, the whole tribe took the train for Netley. Mum had packed some jam sandwiches, lemonade and rusks for the little 'uns. While Doss wheeled Joey in the pram, Floss shepherded the older kids, and Mum held the bag in one hand and the fingers of the little 'uns in the other.

Despite the sombre purpose, it was quite an exciting outing—the family had never taken a trip by train before, and Mum hadn't left town since her courting days, picking violets and bluebells in springtime, blackberries in autumn, in Stakes Wood over Purbrook way.

Just before the train chugged into Netley Station, they caught a glimpse of the military cemetery from the window: a great green sea of white-crested waves rolling up the hill.

'Blimey, how are we going to find Dad amid that lot?' exclaimed Doss. 'Like looking for a needle in a haystack.'

'Someone'll have a plan of the graves,' said Floss confidently. 'The army likes order.'

And so it was. As they made their way up the hill to the garrison chapel, they made enquiries from other visitors. Yes, the chaplain kept a big red ledger with every grave marked. And if they didn't yet have a name, they were allotted a number and letter.

'Private Loveless, B., mmmmm, let me see,' said the chaplain in that peculiar sing-song voice vicars use for preaching. 'Yah. Here he is. Recent. Other ranks. Oh—'

He stopped and peered over the top of his glasses as if confronted by a caravan of gypsies.

'Unsanctified section,' he said coldly. 'Plot 7430 C. Top right corner.'

The ledger banged shut in a cloud of dust. It was like Judgement Day: St Peter barring the way to the pearly gates and pointing down to Hell.

'What's "unsanctified"?' asked Mum.

Nobody knew.

'Maybe they haven't got round to putting a headstone on it,' suggested Doss.

It was only later Floss discovered that suicide didn't

merit a Christian burial. Like Dracula's vampires, Dad's soul would get no rest for all eternity . . .

They located the grave in a special compound with half a dozen others, separated from the mass of neat headstoned plots by a muddy path. It was just a scruffy mound of light-brown soil pitted with flintstone chips. No. 7430 C.

Mum spread out sheets of newspaper—Floss's *Daily Mail*—on the grass surround and they all sat in a circle about Dad's grave. One by one, the kids put posies of primroses on the grave; they'd picked them on the railway verge beside the station. Meanwhile, Doss and Floss tidied up the grave, picking out stones and lumps of clay.

Mum put her hands upon the grave and closed her eyes: she was moving her lips in silent farewell to the man she'd loved, the father of her ten children, the husband she'd never see again. Who would support the family now?

No one said a word while Mum spoke with Dad. But each had their own favourite memories of the shy, gentle, kind father. Only Floss had a different image: of the dark rainy night beside the railway track, the broken broom, the blood-stained rail, the two pitiful bundles.

Mum had banned prayers. Dad wasn't a religious man. But before leaving, they linked hands and Doss led them in a song for Dad.

> There's a long, long trail a-winding
> Into the land of my dreams,
> Where the nightingales are singing
> And a white moon beams.
> There's a long, long night of waiting
> Until my dreams all come true;
> Till the day when I'll be going down
> That long, long trail with you.

They had their picnic by the graveside, sprinkling

crumbs on the mound for Dad; then they made their way back, in time for the five o'clock Portsmouth train.

Mum had done her duty by Dad. She wouldn't go back in a hurry. There'd be time after the war for proper mourning. Now she had to get on, bring up her family, see them safely through the war.

15

I walked into a moon of gold last night,
Across grey sands she seemed to shine so bright.

Wide, wide the sands until I met the sea,
Cradle of moons, yet searchlights followed me.

I asked the moon if creeping round the Zones
She had seen good, or only poor things' bones.

'Pale faces I have seen, unconscious men
Bereft of struggling horror now and then.'
from 'One Night' by Millicent Sutherland

That night, with the children in bed, Floss sat down to write to Jack. She had to pass on the bad news as well as all the latest gossip: Doss's job, her football team, her dancing nights; Mum's spat with the vicar, their Netley outing; her nightly vigils at training hospital, Dad's mate Johnnie Lee, the poems.

She held nothing back about Dad. Jack would understand. She warned him not to mention it in his letters.

Oh, and by the way, his rabbits were well-fed and producing lots of bouncing bunnies.

Before closing, she had a sudden thought. She needed someone to chat about it with. Only her big brother could offer advice. But he wasn't here.

I was thinking . . . What if I come over and join you? 'Course, I'd have to pass the board, cos

87

you're s'posed to be twenty-three. Still, I fooled
them once, didn't I? You lads need someone to
tuck you in at night. My pal Bea at the Royal wrote
to say she's thinking of going overseas too. Maybe
we'll go together.

Do you need my skills? I can make a nice drop
of cocoa, I'm a dab hand at dressing wounds—and
holding legs and arms as the sawbones cuts them
off, just the little everyday jobs.

That's it, Jack. See you in France, eh? I'll be
the big girl in white cap and red cross on my
pinny—your very own Rose of No Man's Land.
Lots of love,
Sis

x x x x x x x

She licked the envelope down and sent it off before
anyone could read it. Her idea of overseas service was a
secret for the moment. Anyway, they'd probably turn her
down.

She wrote a second letter all the same, this time to the
Red Cross headquarters in London that Beatrice Norton
had told her about.

A fortnight later, as she was completing her training
course in Aldershot, she received a letter from Devonshire
House, London. It thanked her for her enquiry and invited
her up for an interview: 12.15 on 1 April. April Fool's
Day!

Not a good omen.

At the stated time, she was standing outside the tall
oak doors of a musty old building in the heart of London.
It was her first ever visit to the capital and she was all of a
tiswas. She had dressed in her VAD uniform—frock hem
two regulation inches above her shoes, showing a daring
glimpse of thick black woolly stockings. Her cheeks were

scrubbed, nails clipped and cleaned, and all other bits of bare flesh smelling healthily of carbolic soap.

'Come.'

She pushed open the door and in she went. How disappointing. She was evidently worth only a little old man. He was sitting behind an enormous dark brown desk, drumming his fingers on a pad of blotting paper.

'Do sit down, nurse,' he said, glancing up at her. 'Mmmmm, Nurse Florence Loveless, I see from your letter. Get through the training all right?'

'Yes, sir. Thank you, sir.'

'Why do you wish to serve overseas?'

'I think I can do more there than here, sir.'

'Do your bit for King and Country, what?'

Floss frowned.

'Not exactly, sir. More for the wounded and dying in this terrible war.'

'You don't approve of the war?'

'Not really, sir. But women aren't normally asked if they approve.'

'What do you know about the situation over there?'

'My brother Jack writes regularly from the Front. Dad's just died of shell-shock. I'm not starry-eyed, if that's what you mean, sir.'

His face showed no emotion. At least he didn't come the old soldier. She was determined to tell the truth— except on one question. And here it came.

'How old are you?'

She knew the minimum age for overseas service was twenty-three, and she was seven years short. But she put a bold face on it and replied that she *was* twenty-three.

The man's bushy eyebrows crept up his forehead and she could feel herself blushing. Then to her relief he wrote down: 'Age 23.'

As she struggled to read his writing upside-down, she saw him add in brackets: 'Apparent age—18.'

So guilty did she feel she couldn't help herself, bursting out, 'Now that you've written it down, sir, it's not 18; I'm coming up for 17.'

He glanced up with a surprised look on his face. She thought she'd blown it. Yet to her relief he rocked back and laughed.

'Nurse, you are a breath of fresh air. If you can cheer me up, you'll surely be a tonic for the troops. I'm going to recommend you for overseas service.'

He smiled warmly.

'Good luck, Nurse Loveless.'

She left the room in a daze. However, as she was walking down the corridor a wild-eyed young man suddenly appeared at her side.

'Are you going to France?' he asked.

She nodded and grinned.

'Then God help you!' he shouted. 'It's hell out there. They're cutting off arms and legs so fast there's no time to clear them away; they're lying all over the place.'

Floss thought he must be off his head, and hurried on. But his words soured what should have been a very sweet moment.

She had agreed to meet Beatrice in a pub by Victoria Station: either to drown her sorrows or to celebrate. Bea had had her grilling in the morning, so neither knew the other's fate.

By the time Floss found her chum in the saloon bar, she was already a couple of sheets to the wind.

'Well, old sport, will you be needing your shea-shicknessh pillsh or not?'

The broad smile on Floss's face told all, and the two women hugged each other happily. That was too much for two city gents at the bar. They upped and left, muttering something about 'damn women' and 'nothing sacred any more.'

'Last orders, gentlemen,' sang out the barman.

'Doesh that mean ladiesh can drink on?' shouted Bea, slurring her words. 'We'll have two large ginsh, my good man, with a teensy-weensy splash of tonic.'

'Something to celebrate, ladies?' the barman asked, handing over the drinks.

'We're off to give new hope to sholdiers in a world of deshpair,' said Bea. 'Cheers, old boy.'

The two friends downed their drinks and, as Bea put it, tootled off for a bite to eat and some champers. What she didn't mention was that they were joining her old friend Millicent Sutherland at the Ritz.

In the taxi on the way, she explained, 'You must meet Millicent, she's a scream. Top hole. Scares the pants off every man she meets.'

Having heard of Bea's pukka friends, Floss asked to be put in the picture.

'Oh, Millicent? The Duchess of Sutherland, to give her proper title. We did our basic training together, though she's twice my age. Millicent was in Belgium, behind the lines, when the Boche invaded, wrote an account of it in *The Times*. Put the wind up a lot of Hun-loving socialites, I can tell you. She knew poor Edith Cavell well, did her darndest to get her off. Lucky not to be shot herself.

'Millicent's a law unto herself, so when the starchy Brits wouldn't accept women doctors, she joined the French Red Cross and took the "Millicent Sutherland Ambulance" to the front with her team of all-women nurses and doctors. Writes poetry too.'

To Floss the next few hours were like a door opening into another world: shiny ballroom floors, glittering chandeliers, fidgety flunkeys opening doors, pulling and pushing chairs, food she'd never even heard of, let alone tasted; and so many glasses of bubbly she soon felt perfectly at ease.

'To the manner born,' as Bea said.

As for the duchess, she was the fiercest, funniest, kindest woman she'd ever met. Not only that, never before had she seen men quake in their boots before such a woman, some kissing her hand, others calling her 'Your Grace'.

By the end of the meal, Bea and Floss were enrolled in the 'Duchess of Sutherland Red Cross Hospital', just outside Calais.

16

'Sudden the air seemed filled with eager breath
Of great Adventurers, released from death.

'And shaking blood from out their eyes and hair
Shouting for further knowledge here and there.

'And as they sped in troops the great guns boomed,
With flashes lightning swift, and dark hordes loomed,

'And phantom shapes of patient warrior bands—
Then more snow fell and shrouded all the lands.'

*   *   *

Now pondering from the moon I turned again,
Over the sands, back to our House of Pain.

from 'One Night' by Millicent Sutherland

Floss soon discovered that the rules of war did not apply
to 'Sister Millicent'. Right from the outset she had bullied
her way through German lines, was on first name terms
with German generals whom she'd known before the
war; and she took her Millicent Sutherland Ambulance
wherever her services were most needed.

Initially, her team of eight nurses were countesses every
one.

Floss could not but admire her energy and devotion to
the wounded. Even so, no one could have been less suited
to the job than the widowed duchess and her aristocratic
chums. They had walked straight out of mansion drawing

rooms, never having soiled their hands, into the filth, the horrors, and the suffering of war. Their only preparation had been first-aid practice on butlers and maids.

Now here they were washing wounds, tearing off rags and clothing soaked in pus, holding basins filled with blood, soothing a soldier's groans and curses, clasping a dying man's rough hand, and working without sleep for days on end.

Having travelled from Brussels by ambulance, charabanc, German-escorted car ('The Germans like well-known people,' she told Floss and Bea), horse and cart, and Shanks's pony ('One very nearly does that in a day's golfing,' she said casually about a two-hundred mile trek across the battlefields), she was back in England. With scarcely a pause for breath, she was raising funds and preparing to take her 'Flying Angels' back again.

To aid her cause, she even found time to write for the papers, give rousing speeches, and squeeze money for drugs, dressings, and disinfectant from her well-oiled connections. At her urging, she had titled ladies all over the country combing their Pekinese dogs three times a day as their contribution to the war effort. The collected combings of fine dog hair could be woven into the lightest of garments to cover the raw backs of wounded soldiers.

Just as important, lords and ladies footed the bill for her new venture: a well-equipped hospital in France, with the dowager duchess as commandant.

The Loveless family's sadness at losing their eldest daughter to the war in France was eased by news that she was under the protection of the well-known war heroine.

'Nothing and no one can harm Sister Millicent's "Flying Angels",' her twin sister announced, calming her mother's anxieties.

94

If the new arrivals in France had expected a grand old chateau or even school building as the hospital, they were sadly let down. As base hospitals go, between front and shoreline, the Duchess of Sutherland's Red Cross Hospital was one of the smartest and best-rigged out—which is like saying a house of sticks was better than a house of straw.

For however good the intention, every hospital was soon flooded by a tidal wave of wounded—wave upon wave upon wave. No warning. Just a fresh convoy of hundreds of men in the middle of the night, sometimes hot on the heels of the last batch. All to fit into fifty beds.

Welcome to war, nurse!

After a particularly big offensive, there could be ten thousand serious casualties in a single day. All to be distributed among the rickety makeshift tents that went by the name of 'base hospitals'. They were terribly tired men, reeking of mud and green-stained bandages, torn apart by shells and shrapnel, pierced right through by machine gun bullets, legs and arms ripped off, lungs choked with gas.

Some shrieked and clawed the air in their agony. Some were already dead, with fixed, empty eyes in waxlike yellow faces.

They had mostly been hurriedly patched up at the casualty clearing stations just behind the lines and sent on for proper treatment. But there was often no room at the base hospitals; so the ambulance crews simply dumped them down on wooden boards, under a rainy sky, until either their turn came . . . or they died.

The blood and the thunder of distant guns mingled with pitiful cries of 'Oh, Mum, help me! Don't let me die!'

But there was nothing anyone could do.

Sister Millicent's hospital was a single marquee, like a

circus Big Top, ringed by four small bell tents. The marquee was for patients, the bell tents took two nurses each, at a pinch.

At the other end of the field was a larger tent for the Camp Commandant; it was flying the duchess's own family pennant.

The hospital had no running water; every drop had to be brought in a bucket from rain barrels and a nearby stream. There was no Sister's Room, just a little trestle table in the centre with a canvas camp stool. Behind that were several boxes that served as medicine chests.

The kitchen was a field camp oven with a trench fire covered by a tarpaulin sheet. The food and drugs stores were hastily knocked together lean-to sheds. A coke stove made out of petrol tins pierced with holes provided the only heating for the ward; the bell tents had no heating at all.

All round the marquee were little wire cages which Floss discovered to her horror were rat traps. But there were no traps for the millions of lice which men brought from the trenches; they had the run of the whole place. Although the nurses cut their hair short and washed themselves every day, the little itchy blighters had no respect for red- or blue-blood flesh: soldier or nurse, skivvy or countess.

No curtains separated dead and dying from the rest, though fortunately the ward was permanently cast in semi-darkness.

At night the marquee was lit by dim electric light, but in the daytime, however dark it was, they used only smelly, smoky oil lamps.

This dingy, gloomy atmosphere was added to by the dark brown and red blankets that helped disguise the blood, pus, urine, and worse which constantly stained them.

At first, Floss most of all feared the constant noise of the battlefront. The shelling seemed so close she imagined a shell would fall on her head at any moment. It made her think of Jack, out there somewhere, braving dangers every day; her sisterly heart went out to him.

Then she thought of Dad, what he must have suffered from the blast, the noise, the heat, the death about him. She heard strange cries of anguish on the wind, like tormented souls of the dead and dying. Was Dad's soul trying to get back to the war? No, she could feel his presence here, fighting the war, helping its victims.

There was so much of her dad in her.

In a way, worse than the boom-boom-boom of battle was the mellow tune played by the bugler each evening: the Last Post.

Just down the coast, on the open slopes by the sea, was the fast-growing cemetery where they buried the dead of the base hospitals.

If there was any tiny consolation for the back-breaking work, it was the uniform, specially designed by the dowager duchess herself and bearing her family crest in place of the red cross. She had spurned the plain Red Cross uniform in favour of an outfit made by her personal haberdasher in Piccadilly.

It consisted of a smart purple and white check dress down to just below the knee ('Let the poor devils glimpse a bit of a lady's leg to give them something to live for,' she used to say), a white linen apron fastened at the back with three buttons, a pretty white cap under which they tucked their hair, and shiny black boots—better than shoes for clambering over rows of stretcher cases and through the clinging mud.

The commandant was a stickler for 'good form', and expected her 'gals' to be 'shipshape and Bristol fashion' at all times. 'Nurse Loveless,' she would boom in a voice that began at the bottom of the scale, zoomed up to the top and back again, 'your apron is not sitting very well.'

She tolerated no crumples, wrinkles, or spots, always showed an example in starched, spanking clean appearance herself, with never a hair out of place. Even the patients had to 'come up to the mark', no matter how ill they were. She permitted no books or paper on beds, smoking only at given times, no ash to be flicked on to her polished wooden floor. And if anyone coughed within her hearing, they had to be given medicine right away to stop that 'unholy row'.

The nurses had to work hard and long, with no days off. A bell rang at six thirty to wake them; after a quick cold breakfast they had to be on the ward by seven thirty. At about ten they had half an hour for a snatched cuppa and change of apron ready for doctor's inspection. They came off duty about nine at night, and were then expected to gather in Her Grace's tent for prayers.

Rather, the commandant read out verses containing 'God' or 'Jesus Christ', often in a despairing, cursing way, like 'Thank Christ for peace!,' 'God help us!' Floss never could make out whether their patron believed in God or not, or had suspended her faith for the duration of the war. If she did believe in God, it was not the one calling on soldiers to 'fight the good fight with all their might'.

By the time Floss flopped into her tent bunk, she was so tired she slept soundly until the bell went next morning. And then she'd pull on her boots and start the daily round once more.

17

The rows of beds,
Each even spaced,
The blanket lying dark against the sheet,
The heavy breathing of the sick,
The fevered voices
Telling of the battle
At the front,
Of Home and Mother.

A quick, light step,
A white-capped figure
Silhouetted by the lantern's flame,
A needly, bearing sleep
And sweet forgetfulness.
A moan—
Then darkness, death.
God rest the valiant soul.

                                        Anon.

One afternoon, in the lull between convoys, Floss sat down at the ward table to write home. She'd promised a letter to let them know she was alive and kicking. And then there was Jack who always longed for news, as much as he was keen to give it.

To save time she'd write one letter to both; she was too tired to bother about sparing them the gory details of her job. Like it or lump it, that's how war was, with all its whopping great warts.

Calais

Dear All,

So here I am finally with half a mo' to spare.
I've been at it for a month that seems a year; no, a
lifetime. And I've seen sights not even meant for
sore eyes. Nothing could have prepared me for
this. It is Hell, absolute Hell. But I wouldn't change
it for the world.

We get casualties straight from the battlefront.
But by the time they get here they've been a few
days festering on the road. So they arrive with
wounds full of mud and bits of cloth, green septic
pits that are a mass of putrid muscle and tissue
rotting away with 'gas gangrene'. I think the worst
is the stink, it's disgusting. We try to clean wounds
up with a red lysol swab. Sometimes it's so dirty,
full of maggots, even lice.

Just recently we've started putting maggots
into wounds because they eat the bad stuff.
Imagine the nasty wriggly things inside someone's
body, eating down to the bone.

I remember my first amputation here. Our
doctor said, 'Go on, nurse, you can help, this one's
dead easy.'

After the operation, I did realize how simple it
is to cut a hand or arm off. I stand next to our
woman doctor, lift the amputated arm or leg with
my forceps and drop it—plop!—into the slop
bucket.

See, simple—though more dead than easy.

It's funny how strong men want to hold your
hand during these moments. They need contact
with another life. It's sad when someone dies and
you've been holding their hand, maybe patted it to

give them courage. So often they look up at me and say, 'You remind me of my mother'—who'd be three times my age. God—I'm only sixteen— maybe war has aged me! But I do feel proud when they say that.

I nursed a young boy who kept crying for his mummy. He had dreadful wounds, all inside him, tied up with tubes that ran into a bucket beneath his bed. He was put up against the marquee door, because anyone likely to die is always put there so's he can be taken out without any fuss. Nonetheless, he seemed to have turned the corner when the home convoy officer came in.

'We've one place left in the convoy,' he said; 'we'll take this lad.'

I objected as strongly as I could, asking for a few more days for him to get up his strength for the sea crossing. But no, they took him off—had to fill their quota. Later I heard he did see his mummy, and then died. Shame, isn't it? So unnecessary too.

We had a giant of a Scots sergeant in with a very mud-spattered, blood-stained tunic. I cut off his uniform, even his tartan kilt, and gave him a blanket bath; I could see he was dreadfully embarrassed to have a girl bathe him, and he was in awful pain, but not a peep. When he was getting better, I read him out a bit from the paper about heartless Germans killing prisoners. And he went all quiet, his face turned to stone; in a flash, I realized he must have done the same. He had such a beautiful deep voice and used to cheer everyone up with Scottish songs, 'Ye Banks and Braes', 'Loch Lomond', and 'Bonnie Mary of Argyle'. One day I asked him to sing 'Annie Laurie'. But he just shook his head. 'Oh, go on,' I said. When he refused I realized the song must stir up painful memories for him. Then one morning I was doing some messy dressings when I heard his voice, very soft, singing 'Annie Laurie', and I knew he was singing it to help me. He never sang it again.

One last case I must tell you about, it so sticks in my mind. We'd had a young fellow with us for some time. He was more sick than he knew, being blind and full of gangrene. One day, he asked me 'When will they take off my bandages so that I can see?' I didn't know what to say. He went on with a laugh, 'Why, I haven't ever seen you, nurse.' Later that day, the MO told him he was blind and couldn't be cured. That evening, he called for me, 'Nurse Loveless, please come and sit with me.' I sat beside him; there was a bit of a draught blowing through the door. He sighed and murmured, 'You know I'm blind for good?'

'Yes,' I answered, taking one of his hands in mine. He said he was hungry, so I fed him hot buttered toast and warm sweet milk. It was hard to find his mouth in the dark, and he laughed, a funny little husky laugh, when the crumbs went up his nose.

'It will be a month tomorrow since I was hit,' he said as he crunched the last piece of toast. 'All the time before now seems like a different life. Queer, ain't it?' Then he added, and again gave that husky little laugh, 'I say, nurse, you won't forget my early morning tea, will you. You know, you did forget it yesterday.' With those words he reached his hand towards me, his way of discovering if I was offended.

He died yesterday morning, the young blind

chap I'd become so fond of. That evening, there was a little concert and the men sang,

> 'There's a long, long trail a-winding,
> Into the land of my dreams,
> Where the nightingales are singing,
> And the pale moon gleams.'

Of course, it reminded me of us all singing round Dad's grave, and I shed a little tear. And there by the door was an empty bed, clean and fresh, a set of pyjamas beneath the pillows, waiting for the next patient.

Well, I guess that will give you a glimpse of my work. A man comes in, you grow fond of him, do what you can to comfort him, and he dies. You move on. Sad, isn't it? That's war.

I send you all my love,

Floss

x x x x x x x

18

Forward, brave and dauntless
Daughters of this earth,
Let your dormant talents
Spring to glorious birth.

Children, toiling sisters,
Cry, and never rest;
Answer! We shall help you
Coming to our best.

Forward, fighting evils,
Deborahs, awake!
Up! And help your sisters
Victims at life's stake.
from 'Forward, Ever Forward' by Margaret O'Shea

Portsmouth 1 June 1917

Dear Sister Floss,

I'm the muggins who has to write
(groan, groan). Mum's too busy with housework,
the kids all have stiff fingers. There's no news
anyway, life goes on just the same. Ta for your
letter. You do enjoy an easy life, sitting around all
day holding hands with soldiers, drinking tea, no
one to boss you about. Let's have more horror
stories of blood-dripping legs, stinking sores,
dying men. Just the job to tell the kids at bedtime
(ha-ha, only kidding).

I do envy you, being so free. Give me your

104

lady toffs any day to the nosy old busybodies who watch us all the time. Old Ha-Ha's bad enough, but the dockyard's taken on female bobbies to keep an eye on us, break up strikes, search and strip us—hoping to find fags or booze. They're the usual la-di-da killjoys putting a stop to our fun, forcing their silly ideas down our throats. They reckon we need a 'better class' of woman over us because, 'like Tommy, we don't want our own kind in charge'. Ugh!

Ha-Ha laid on a series of lunchtime lectures for us—to teach us about life. Sometimes they're a real scream, especially when they're on sex and suchlike 'rude' matters. They must think we don't know where babies come from. The other day we had some old biddy, our very own special medical officer, come to tell us about her new handbook for welfare officers—the *Health of Working Girls*; she claims it's based on her own observations (in the zoo, more like!). This is what I remember the silly old bat saying:

'Now then, girls, I feel compelled to point out two areas of special concern: self-abuse (at first we had no idea what she meant, then someone said it was "fiddling with yourself", so we cottoned on and listened more closely) and the sexual consequences of drinking. By describing the symptoms of self-abuse I may help you recognize and help the sufferers. They are usually pale, dull-eyed with dark rings round the eyes.' She couldn't understand why we roared with laughter, pointing to Mrs Ha-Ha whom she'd described to a tee!

'They are often morose and shy and seem unable to look one straight in the face. It is our

105

duty to help as much as possible in the way of cold baths, swimming lessons, and healthy outdoor amusements (shouts of ''shooting Germans'' and ''marching with the Suffragettes''), and cutting out red meat, tea and coffee (shouts of ''drink gin and stout instead!'').'

She ranted on, but, the good bits over, we carried on chatting among ourselves, occasionally blowing raspberries and telling her to 'go and abuse herself'. Such sideshows certainly liven up our dinner hour. When will they learn that we know far more about sex than those repressed old maids ever will? Or that being lectured to by some prig just gets up our noses and makes us do the opposite.

Small wonder we grab what fun we can when we see so many young men being killed or coming home with no legs, faces, or brains!

Another thing those busybodies are scared of is us getting the vote. You'll be glad to know that I do my bit selling literature, marching, even speaking on street corners. Mum came along too the other day; she was a bit shy at first, but when some docker started chucking tomatoes at me, she bashed him one with Joey's pram, doubled him up. Good old Mum: we'll make a rebel of her yet.

Even the ex-Prime Minister Mr Asquith has come out in favour of us getting a 'measure' of suffrage. As he says, 'How can we carry on the War without them?' I think he's begun to change his tune ever since his son Raymond was killed in action. It was all over the papers.

Did you know Lord Kitchener copped it last year? His ship was sunk by a mine. 'Got his just deserts,' Mum reckons, 'for bullying all those poor youngsters like Jack into enlisting.' Well, his country certainly doesn't need him any more! This war is sweeping away the old order, Flo. And it's us women who're showing a lead.

Where will it all end? When all the men kill each other there'll be only us women left. We'll be in charge.

Don't think we have it easy at home. Only the other day German bombers appeared in the sky over Portsmouth; they looked and sounded like buzzing gnats. We all rushed up to the workshop roof and watched the bombs fall—some into the sea, some on the town. From what I hear they killed some horses in Commercial Road, and they turned Fratton and North End into rivers of broken glass. But no one lost their lives. Makes you wonder though: England isn't an island any more.

Another exciting moment was seeing a Zeppelin brought down. One bright morning this giant sausage appears over Portsdown Hill; they reckon it was up to no good, taking photos of our forts along the hilltop. It must have got too close, cos suddenly the big guns opened up from Fort Purbrook, tore through the sausage skin and the whole lot went up in flames. I felt a bit sorry for the crew. Not a nice way to go.

'Course, on Sunday we were all up on the Hill searching for souvenirs. All I got was a bit of charred fabric; but Maisie Bates found an old leather boot—she swore it came from the German pilot. 'One Jerry less,' she said.

With my four quid a week, I bought myself a new football outfit, and some lipstick, rouge, and powder for Mum. She swore not to use it: 'I've no one to tart myself up for apart from Toto the new dog (we called him Toto after Dorothy's dog in the *Wonderful Wizard of Oz*) and old Ebenezer the rentman.' Funny though, when I came in late the other night, all the kids were in bed and I could hear someone talking in the kitchen. I crept in and there was Mum all done up to the nines, holding Dad's picture up to her face. She was crying, 'Bert, oh Bert,' over and over again, as if her calling would somehow bring him back.

Mind you, I'm not sure Dad would approve of Mum in make-up.

That's about all the news from the home front. The kids send their love; Mum says give you a great big kiss. She's really very proud of her lovely smelly 'Rose'. Come home soon.
Your loving sister,
Dossie x x x x x
PS Our old headmaster Mr Cleal has gone off to 'do his bit'—Maybe you'll bump into him on the operating table (we live in hope!).

20 June   Pte Jack Loveless   Passchendaele
Dear Sis,

How are you, Sister Florence? By my reckoning we're only a few miles apart, you by the sea, me stuck in a trench beside the River Lys. What lovely rolling downlands. Maybe I'll pop over to see you when I'm stood down.

This is just a quickie between 'offensives'. We're getting ready for the Big Push (yet another!) —so expect a few more hospital visitors soon. True, there *is* a massive build-up ready to shove Jerry back. We're going to launch our secret weapon: the tank. That'll finish 'em off (some hope). Our officers are so sure of victory they've

ordered us to walk, *not run*, towards enemy lines
when the balloon goes up. Perhaps it doesn't hurt
so much catching a bullet on the run!

4 July same place
Didn't have a chance to post my letter. The Push
has started . . . and we're back where we were, far
more dead than alive. Before the offensive we had
a new draft of seventeen officers come in to plug
the gaps. I give them all two months at the most.
Some'll get hit before they know where they are,
some'll go on leave and never return, some'll go
sick, and some'll be posted to less dangerous
work. Guess who turned up like a bad penny! Old
Gingernob Cleal, accompanied by his batman
Hanging Judge Jeffries, our old PT master.

    It was Cleal who gave the order 'Walk, not
run!' just as he used to in the playground. And
what happened? As he dodged down in the
trenches, we went over the top and got mown
down like grass in a hayfield. Anyone who wasn't
hit on that day, first of July, must have had angel's
wings on his back. I'd only gone a couple of yards,
stepping over barbed wire, when I got a bullet in
my water bottle and another in the ankle. The
shelling was so bad it was like being swept about
like dandelion fluff on a windy day. I crawled as
best I could until I fell into a shell hole. Right at the
bottom was Mr Jeffries with his head hanging off!

    'You won't be needing your water bottle now,
sir,' I says. I was so thirsty from loss of blood, I
took a darn good swig . . . but it was full of rum
and made me spew my guts up.

    Next thing I know I wake up at casualty station
and this orderly's nicking my watch. I'm too weak

to do anything about it. I'm writing this now in awful pain as I lie in the luggage rack of an ambulance train. They say I need urgent surgery if they're to save my foot. So it doesn't sound as if I'll play for Pompey again, does it? Well, I might eventually end up in your care. I do hope so.

Lots of love,

Your loving brother Jack x x x x x x x

19

Oh, guns of France,
Be still, you crash in vain . . .
Heavily up the south wind throb
Dull dreams of pain . . .

Be still, be still, south wind, lest your
Blowing should bring the rain . . .
We'll lie very quiet on Hurt Hill
And sleep once again.

Oh, we'll lie quite still, nor listen nor look,
While the earth's bounds reel and shake,
Lest, battered too long, our walls and we
Should break . . . should break.
from 'Picnic, July 1917' by Rose Macaulay

Shortly after receiving the two letters, Floss was doing her evening rounds when she heard the drone of planes. It was such a familiar sound—ours flying in, theirs flying out—that she gave it no further thought.

'German bombers,' remarked a one-legged corporal to no one in particular.

'They won't touch us,' said Bea loudly to calm any fears. She was sharing night duty with Floss. 'There's a lovely full moon, so they can't miss the big red crosses painted on our roof.'

Famous last words.

First came the engine roar overhead, then the whine and whistle, last of all the deafening explosion. At once the electric lamps all went out, and the whole marquee shook violently as if some ogre had it by the scruff of the neck. Anyone standing up was knocked sprawling on the floor as the entire ward was turned upside down. A strong wind tore through the canvas walls.

For several moments panic reigned: shouts, screams, groans, tinkling glass, crashing wooden chests, the screech of castors over floorboards as beds were buffeted about.

It was Bea who reacted first. She pulled herself groggily to her feet and felt for Floss's shoulder, shaking her gently.

'Are you all right?'

Hearing a shaky reply, she muttered, 'I'll fetch some oil lamps; you take care of the men.'

As Bea groped her way towards the moonlight shining through the door flap, Floss hoisted her body off the floor, resting on the iron arm of the upturned trestle table.

'Be calm,' she quoted from her nursing manual. 'Don't show fear, keep control at all times.'

From outside the marquee came the most unearthly screams, like the wailing of a thousand banshees. She guessed it was the horses tethered close to the bell tents. A bomb must have landed near them. She'd never heard a horse scream before; it was the most heart-rending noise she'd ever known.

'Keep calm,' she said loudly, desperately trying to control her own trembling voice. 'In half a mo, Nurse Norton will be back with hurricane lamps. Then we'll be able to take stock. We'll have a roll call to make sure everyone's OK.'

'Bed 1.'

'Present, Nurse.'

'Bed 2.'

'Still in one piece, Nurse.'

'Bed 3.'

'Here,' came a wobbly voice from underneath the bed. 'Bed 4.'

'I need a hand to get back into bed. Otherwise I'm fine, thank you, Nurse.'

'Right, hold on Bed No. 4. I'll be with you in a tick.'

So it continued down to Bed 19. No one was badly hurt. Just bumps, disconnected tubes, and a few cuts from flying glass.

But what with the shock and the horses' screeching, everyone's nerves were on edge.

'Never mind us,' said one man. 'Get someone to put those bloody beasts out of their misery.'

From force of habit, Floss said sharply, 'No swearing please! Commandant's rules. We'll deal with the dumb animals, all in good time.'

By the time Bea returned with the oil lamps, Floss had helped the fallen patient back into bed and straightened table and chairs. Most of the men, especially those fresh from the trenches, were trembling uncontrollably. She reflected that, in a crisis, women were the stronger; men folded more easily.

Behind Bea came the duchess, visibly shaken in the half-light, but firmly in control of herself and the situation.

'Now, you men, no damage?'

She cut an odd figure—like the warrior queen Boadicea, very tall and gaunt, and unusually unkempt. With her long grey hair flying about her, she looked fiercer than ever, fixing any groaning man with one of her stares that immediately stilled his noise.

She was clearly not amused.

'The bounders! How dare they bomb the Red Cross. It's against the rules of war. I'll write to the Kaiser himself, the dashed cheek of it. I'll make him pay for this. It just isn't cricket!'

As she stormed on about Kaiser Bill, she made her way round the beds, swinging her lamp to and fro, patting, tucking, reconnecting, reassuring each man. When she'd done, she muttered hoarsely to her two nurses.

'The blighters have done us a mischief. All the bell tents blown to Kingdom Come—four nurses have bought it, barely a trace of them left on God's earth. Lucky we had no patient lying outside.'

A pained tone came into her voice.

'Poor old gee-gees took a direct hit. Nurse Norton, go and do the decent thing, will you; put them out of their misery. We'll bury them in the morning.'

She handed Bea her revolver—and off went the doctor's daughter as if it was all in a night's work.

'The Hun has destroyed our stores,' continued Her Grace. 'In the morning, Nurse Loveless, you and Nurse Norton are to go for supplies. Take the ambulance. It'll be a while before we're back on our feet. Carry on.'

She swept out, hair streaming behind her. In the half light, Floss noticed her bare feet had left blood-stained prints at every step. That was typical of the grand dame: patients came first, her own safety second. Or perhaps she hadn't even noticed.

Which four of Floss's nursing friends had been killed? Such was the regularity of death she didn't even dwell long on the loss. At least, they seem not to have suffered. There were plenty of nurses' graves alongside those of soldiers at the cemetery down the hill; so she knew that a Red Cross uniform was no protection against death.

Five single shots from outside put an end to the awful shrieks. Now all was still.

Floss and Bea hardly got any rest that night as they patrolled the ward, calming the bomb-shocked patients. And as the new day dawned—such a glorious sunny daybreak—they saw the full extent of the Devil's

114

handiwork. Where the nurses' tents had stood was a single deep hole full of nothing but red earth, worms, and a black puddle.

Where had the four bodies gone? Down the throat of Thor, the god of war. All the nurses' scant belongings had blown away. The stores were flattened: the wooden walls had fallen in, the contents had tumbled out. All over the ground lay a jumble of cotton wool, gauze, swabs, and rolls of bandages. Liquid from smashed bottles had coagulated into one slimy, greeny-violet pool: a mixture of olive oil, iodine, lysol, morphine, castor oil, and carbolic 20.

What a stink! Even the jars of live maggots had spilled out their contents; they were now feeding off less tasty titbits than human flesh.

The only parts of the hospital left were the marquee at one end and the commandant's quarters at the other. All that remained in the middle was a forlorn cast-iron oven, standing there like a serene black Buddha: indestructible, but useless for any practical purpose.

First things first. The remaining half of the staff dug a pit for the five dead horses, while Her Grace marched off towards the woods in search of bodies. When she returned, she was dragging what looked like a sack of knobbly potatoes—bits and stumps she'd found in trees and flower beds over a hundred yards away.

By that time a small convoy of ambulances was driving into the pitted field.

'Ah, dear FANY riding to the rescue,' sighed Bea.

The First Aid Nursing Yeomanry (FANY) prided itself on being tough and fearless. They had to be: the FANY women not only drove their battered ambulances over rough, upturned soil, they had to carry heavy stretchers and load sad remnants of once-strong men on and off their vehicles.

Her Grace oversaw the transfer of her patients to other hospitals around the Pas de Calais, most to the main base hospital at Etaples. She shook hands with those who had a hand and wished them well, 'Chin-chin, old chum. We shall rise again from the ashes, like the Phoenix, I give you my word.'

If she grieved over the destruction of her good work, she didn't show it. Her jaw jutted out defiantly as she plotted a new campaign for funds and an even grander 'Duchess of Sutherland Hospital'.

As she stalked off to her tent, Floss heard her muttering, 'Pity about the horses . . . '

20

A mile or two outside the town
The silent forests stand; that spread
Down where the road has faded brown
And the pale leaves fall silver red,
Thick underfoot in rise and swell
Damp with old rains and sweet to smell,
Red underfoot, red overhead.

The road is white beneath the moon.
Go on until the dawn is new,
And you may meet the strange dragoon
And he may stop to ride with you. . . .

from 'Brussels, 1919' by Carola Oman

With a letter from Millicent Sutherland as their only passport through the war zones, Bea and Floss set off at midday in the ambulance. Bea was at the wheel, as cheerful as ever despite the tragedy. Floss had had no more than rough and ready driving instruction; but she would watch and learn from Bea.

The vehicle was an old cattle truck converted into an ambulance suited to rutted roads. The two women sat up front in the open; at their back was a covered wagon painted with a large red cross on sides, roof, and back. To 'protect' them from shells and the elements, both wore army helmets and khaki overalls.

Their mission was to 'beg, borrow, or buy' a fresh supply of drugs, dressings, and medicines from whatever hospital would help. Until they returned, the Millicent

117

Sutherland Hospital was closed till further notice. Its patron had gone hot foot to England for more funds.

As for her 'gals', they were to gain supplies 'on her good name'. She had absolutely no doubt that, such was her reputation, mere mention of her name and title would have hospital superintendents falling over themselves to help.

Sadly, supplies were running low everywhere and even the duchess's good name cut no ice with hard-pressed doctors or the army.

'Sorry, miss, we haven't enough for ourselves,' was the common response.

So they had to drive further, down dusty, shell-pocked roads, through ruined French villages and towns that ran parallel with the front: Messines, Givenchy, Vimy, Arras. Their route was to the south; to the north and west were the German lines.

At Arras, they came away empty-handed, as usual. But a field orderly fresh from the battlefield gave them some helpful advice.

'Further down, in Picardy, the route towards the Somme and St Quentin has become a wasteland; it's been fought over, toing and froing, for two years now. But in the last month we've shoved Jerry back a mile or so. With any luck you'll find an abandoned casualty station with stocks intact. Take what you can.'

True enough, as they drove out of Arras they entered a land that resembled the surface of the moon; it was certainly like nothing on earth, a place where human beings had lived and breathed, where farmers had once ploughed and harvested the fields, where men and women had built and prayed in churches, where little children had once played, sung, and laughed.

No laughter now lightened the cheerless land.

Just deserted, crumbling stone buildings, stunted black

118

trees that from a distance looked for all the world like screaming men caught in the agony of death. The once-neat fields were now rutted with trenches and craters, where nothing but hardy weeds and wild flowers struggled through the mire. It was as if a volcano had erupted, spewing its lava across the slopes and plains, killing all life in its path.

In this horrific graveyard that stretched as far as the eye could see, they passed overturned trucks and gun carriages, the carcasses of horses and, to their surprise, rotting human corpses.

There were hundreds and hundreds, far too many for a Christian burial. In any case, men once buried were often tossed up again as war disturbed their rest. Their faces had nothing human about them: these 'moon men' matched the moon landscape. Their cheeks were hollow, beards long, clothes thick with dust and mud. Here and there open wounds had spilled dark-red blood on pale, yellowish skin.

It was hard to tell friend from foe; they were all jumbled up, lying like comrades, side by side.

What looked like mounds of earth along the ruined ramparts of a ditch often turned out to be human remains. British, French, German? Who knew? It was impossible to recognize nationality either from their clothes covered by filth, or from their headgear, for they were all bareheaded; or from their weapons, for they had no rifles, or their hands rested lightly on something they had dragged along, a shapeless, sticky mess like rotting fish.

All these corpses were as alike as if they were naked, yet they were clad in the same uniform of misery and filth. It was the end of time, the end of everything.

As they drove their ambulance through this valley of death, the two women could hear guns rumbling in the distance, feel the ground trembling, smell the battlesmoke wafting towards them on the breeze, filling the air with dust that scorched throat and nostrils. The heat was overpowering and they were attacked by huge black flies and greenbottles—not content with feeding off dead flesh. The entire land gave off a rotting smell that made them both feel sick.

It was a relief to reach the town of Péronne where human beings were walking about the ruins, carrying on their lives as if no soldier of any nation had swept through their homes, shooting each other—and anyone who got in their way.

The two friends halted at dusk in the shadow of a lovely old cathedral that had miraculously escaped serious damage. It was a peaceful shrine amidst the horrors of war that raged beyond its tall walls.

The two women entered the great halls of stone without a word. It was cool and quiet, and smelt sweetly of incense and candles. The few worshippers paid them no attention. In a dim corner gleamed a little red light where two old women were kneeling, their heads covered by black scarves.

The white altar glimmered in the gloom; only the red in the clothes of the figures depicted on it was visible— dimmed by age. There was a dark brown organ in an alcove. It lay silent, yet seemed to give out soft music to calm all earthly cares.

The stained glass windows loomed darkly above them, yet suddenly one colour came into its own and shone out in the halo around the head of a saint. The late summer sun had also thrown a yellow-and-red patch upon the stone aisle, a long ray of light that pierced the mist of dust and dreams.

The Holy Ghost was present in the cathedral—in the form of a dove that hung, with outstretched wings, above the nave. Far below strayed the two women, lost in the vastness.

'One should never stand still in a cathedral,' whispered Bea in a hollow voice that echoed round the stone walls. 'No, one should walk round as one gazes about. Then one realizes how one harmony melts into another.'

She sank down on one knee, head bowed in prayer.

How strange. Floss had never heard her companion mention God before, nor seen her say her prayers. She left her to her own thoughts and walked on, staring up and around in awe. How beautiful and how restful the place was. Yet there was something wrong, something that made her feel uneasy.

'I know,' she breathed. 'It's the reminder of torment and dying. It's everywhere.'

She looked up at the leering gargoyles jutting out of the walls, such a cruel look on their ugly faces; her gaze was drawn to the huge statue of Christ nailed by his hands and feet to a cross, a crown of thorns dripping blood from his head. On one wall was a picture of St Sebastian, his pale naked body pierced by a dozen arrows.

'Why do men turn God's church into a house of pain?' she asked herself.

After spending the night in the back of their dusty truck, sleeping on canvas stretchers, the two women bought rolls, butter, and cheese in one of the few remaining shops, and set off towards St Quentin which marked the front line. The shopkeeper told Bea, who spoke French, that their best bet for medical supplies lay in the abandoned first-aid posts attached to the trenches—if they hadn't been raided by local people for 'souvenirs' . . .

Out of Heaven into Hell . . .

21

There will come soft rains and the smell of the ground,
And swallows calling with their shimmering sound;

And frogs in the pools singing at night,
And wild-plum trees in tremulous white;

Robins will wear their feathery fire
Whistling their whims on a low fence-wire;

And not one will know of the war, not one
Will care at last when it is done.

Not one would mind, neither bird nor tree,
If mankind perished utterly;

And Spring herself, when she woke at dawn,
Would scarcely know that we were gone.
     'There Will Come Soft Rains' by Sara Teasdale

A short distance out of Péronne, the track came to an abrupt end. Ahead was soil soaked in the blood of the thousands who fell on the first day of the Battle of the Somme, the year before.

'Jack was here,' Floss murmured to her companion, staring about her in disbelief. 'He said they were made to line up as if on parade and then march off for Berlin. They got no more than a few yards, blown to bits, hung out to dry on the barbed wire, ground to pulp like apples in a cider press. Poor devils, they were lambs to the slaughter led by Judas goats.'

Bea nodded in sympathy, recalling her own dead brother and fiancé.

'Still, he's safe and, with any luck, will be on his way back to Blighty. No more war for him.'

She stopped the engine and started to climb down from the stranded vehicle.

'Come on, old bean, end of the road.'

They set off for the battlefield, clambering over upturned soil towards the nearest dug-out. An entire trench system spread out before them like a giant worm's burrow. What a waste of all that digging!

Floss led the way, stomping along in her big army boots until they reached the first trench. She helped Bea down into the crumbling hideaway, and together they edged warily along the underground pathway, unable to see above the parapet. The mud trench soon narrowed and deepened, so that the walls seemed to be steadily closing in on them. They had to wriggle a path for themselves into a second trench.

'What a blooming nuisance,' grumbled Floss. 'We'll have to go further. Looks like grave robbers have been at work, taking everything they can sell.'

They pressed on and eventually came to a crooked signboard marked Trench 97. A fallen oak had twisted its great bulk across the entrance, pinning down a corpse whose head and legs were buried in the ground. Dirty water covered the frigid remains, slimy and pale, like the belly of a stranded crocodile.

To progress further they had to plunge their hands up to the wrists into the mud of the wall, and haul themselves over the two twisted bodies.

Further along the trench, earthy bodies were squatting with chins on knees or leaning against the wall as straight and silent as the rifles that lay beside them. The presence of guns told the women that the corpses had stood undisturbed since their final moments.

Some of the blood-spattered faces were turned towards the visitors, a twisted look of curiosity on their fixed features.

Despite the sun in the heavens above, here in the depths of hell the water through which they had to wade was as thick as syrup and cold as ice. In places they felt bodies squirm beneath their feet as they trod over a human carpet. Both gave a gasp of terror as a sudden movement or stream of bubbles in the water signalled life—not of soldiers, but of water rats feeding off dead flesh, vexed at being disturbed.

Round a sharp bend they suddenly came upon what they were looking for: a trench leading back to what had once been a first-aid post. Judging by the yawning emptiness and well-stocked medicine chests, the men had had no chance of first aid or any other help.

'It's no good to them now,' remarked Bea. 'We're only robbing Peter to save Paul; it's not as if we're going to flog the stuff.'

They set to work, stuffing pockets and pouches with whatever came to hand: rolls of bandages, wads of cotton wool, swabs and gauze, bottles of pink, blue, and green liquid. They didn't bother even to read the labels. It would all come in handy. But they would have to make several trips for the bulky medicine chests, most still unopened.

It was an exhausting job in the filth and stink of the trenches, with swarms of flies and lice attacking them, and bloated grey rats scuttling away to safety. By late afternoon, however, they had loaded up the ambulance until there was no more space.

'There, Millicent will be pleased,' said Bea with a sigh. 'And it hasn't cost her a penny. I can't wait to get back to Péronne, and soak myself in a hot bathtub. Before I do anything else, I've got to rid myself of this stench, mud, and lice.'

'With any luck, we should be there by seven if we step on it,' said Floss. 'I do hope you can find the way back.'

What with the criss-crossing of tracks, the stunted hedgerows and frequent craters, direction was going to be more luck than judgement without a compass. But, as it turned out, direction wasn't their worry.

They hadn't driven more than fifty yards when they ran over some strands of barbed wire. The sudden hiss of escaping air told them the worst.

'Oh, blow and bother!' exclaimed Bea. 'That's blown it; we've only got one spare. I hope they haven't both gone for a burton.'

They jumped down and dashed round the back, their groans mingling with the approaching war thunder. The two back tyres were as flat as a pancake, tangled up with sharp metal burrs.

No patch and pump job could repair the chewed-up rubber.

They were stuck, two stray roses in No Man's Land.

'Now what?' asked Floss, aware of the stupidity of her question.

They had come all this way, gained the supplies they needed and were on the return leg. Then, all at once: phut, pop, bang!

What with the gunfire ahead and behind them, they felt like rats caught in a trap. Which way out? Which side was ours?

Bea surprised her companion. She sank down on the stepboard, put her head in her hands and wept. Floss had always thought her as hard as nails, incapable of tears.

'Come on, lovey,' said Floss softly. 'Let's stride out for the nearest town. We can hire a car, buy two new tyres, and come back tomorrow morning for our precious ambulance.'

'*If* it's still here,' whined Bea through her sobs.

All the same, she hauled herself up and trudged off beside her friend. Although Floss led the way, she actually had no clue as to which way to go, though she didn't let on. Not that it mattered. For they hadn't gone far when a shell whistled overhead and crashed into the ground before them, showering them both with damp earth.

'Quick, Bea, back to the ambulance,' shouted Floss frantically.

They rushed back to the truck, flung open the back doors and clambered in. And there they sat, squashed between their treasure chests and stretchers, desperately hoping the battle would pass them by.

As the minutes ticked by, Bea slowly regained her spirit, and although she wasn't exactly cheerful, she did start to spout as she gazed out at the land around. Floss didn't interrupt her, wondering if her gushing words were the product of shattered nerves.

'I love Nature. At home I used to paint flowers and trees at this time of year. Dad used to say, ''You'd paint all of Nature's bounty your eyelashes could encircle.'' Even amid the ugliness of war you can find beauty. See how the meadows take on a bluish tinge from the rising mist on the brink of that stream over there. Look over there—the autumn crocus in the tangled grass.'

She would have continued her musings had not a shell suddenly torn apart her bed of early autumn crocuses. Gunfire was growing louder and, all at once, they caught the sound of voices on the wind, too far off to make out the words.

They held their breath. In the distance, they suddenly caught sight of soldiers, bayonets fixed, scores of them, running towards them. They could tell they were the enemy by their uniforms: the spiked helmets, field-grey tunics, and long calf-length boots.

Neither had ever seen a Hun before, but they had read in the newspaper a few months earlier that the Germans were no longer taking prisoners . . .

'This is it, old chum,' said Bea grimly. 'Chin-chin, nah-poo, toodle-oo, goodbye.'

Images of Nurse Cavell, Jack, Dad, Mum, and the kids flashed through Floss's mind as she waited for a bayonet to be thrust through her.

22

The moon had a courtyard
into which they shoved cannons.
The sun had a light
of which they made torches.
The field was filled with corn
of which they made scrap.

The night had a coat
from which they cut camouflage.
The man had a fist
of which they made bombs.
The woman had a lap
which they named a tavern.

The children had clear vision
they knew their enemy
and made use of everything.

'The Enemy' by Bettina Wegner, trans. by Agnes Stein

Two young soldiers came rushing to the rear of the ambulance, bayonets at the ready—as if they would run through the occupants, no questions asked.

Both women thought their last moment had come. They screwed tight their eyes, awaiting the cold steel in chest or belly. When nothing happened, they squinted down at the men: was there hope yet?

The soldiers had halted, uncertain, listening out for the roar of a car engine.

As a long black sedan drove up, a tall, elegant Prussian

officer slowly descended. The two women could scarcely believe their eyes. Here was a man they thought existed only on British recruiting posters.

He was dressed immaculately, as if he'd just emerged from company headquarters. His belt and boots shone like conkers, he sported a monocle in one eye, a cane walking stick in his hand, and a cigarette holder in one corner of his mouth.

If his appearance surprised them, his first words took them aback.

'Ah, Dr Livingstone, I presume!'

In perfect English.

Bea rose to the occasion. This high-ranking officer with the bored expression and drawl was clearly someone of her own station.

'This isn't darkest Africa, sir,' she snapped. 'I am Red Cross Nurse Beatrice Norton, my friend is Red Cross Nurse Florence Loveless. By the rules of war we . . . '

'Yes, yes, dear ladies, spare me the riot act. When I was at Oxford I found the English lady a bore and battleaxe in equal measure; she didn't know her place in gentlemen's society.'

Bea's blood was up.

'And it is brutish cads like you who would confine women to the home, polishing your boots and breeding your offspring.'

Floss looked on anxiously. To insult a German officer, even if they were nurses, risked instant death. Not for the first time she reflected that the upper classes formed a closer bond with each other than with their own people. But to her relief, the young monocled officer rocked back on his heels and roared with laughter.

'By the rules of war,' he finally spluttered, 'I could have you shot. First you are dressed as army men, not nurses—so how am I to know what you are? Second,

129

you are using your Red Cross as cover for stealing contraband.'

Turning to the two soldiers, he barked an order in German, presumably for them to search the van.

''Raus, 'raus!' screamed one of the soldiers to the two women, pushing them out with the butt of his rifle.

'I regret to say I must treat you as prisoners of war,' continued the former Oxford student. 'I trust you won't eat too much as our rations are frugal. All your fault, I'm sure.

'However, I have a proposition. The German medical service has a motto: "The wounded always come first", and I've an awful lot of wounded in St Quentin. I'm short of help and supplies. If you would like to do your comrades-in-distress a good turn . . . '

After a moment's silence, Bea grumbled, 'We don't seem to have much choice.'

He smiled and bowed graciously.

'No, otherwise I shall shoot you.'

It hardly needed much reflection. If they could help relieve suffering—anyone's suffering—it was their duty as Red Cross nurses to do so.

'All right, we'll do our best.'

He bowed again, then turned to his sergeant, pointing to the punctured tyres. They caught the words St Quentin and 'Kirche', which Bea said meant 'church'; they gathered that the Germans would patch up the tyres and drive the ambulance to the church-hospital in the French town.

'Jump in, dear ladies,' invited the officer, holding open the passenger door of his dusty car. 'I'll take you poppets there myself. My wounded are holed up in an old church.'

His driver made a wide detour of the battlefield before linking up with a bumpy country road. On the way the officer seemed pleased to air his English and lecture the prisoners.

'I had to quit Oxford before my Finals—dashed bad luck! The war, don't you know. Still, I'm honoured to serve God, Kaiser, and Fatherland. Our cause is just, blessed by God; victory will be ours. You English are so arrogant: you think you can grab two thirds of the world, plunder and kill whoever stands in your way in Africa and Asia. Did we object to your expansion? Not a bit.

'Yet the moment overcrowded Germany shifts its borders a few miles, you come rushing in to drive us back . . . Do you see this?'

He tweaked his necktie bearing a badge that said '*Gott strafe England*'.

'God punish England!' he explained. 'The English are such bullies and hypocrites. Far worse than the lily-livered French and barbaric Russians!'

They could see that his time in England had not developed any love of the country in him. Since there was no point arguing—he did hold their lives in his hands— they sat glumly, bouncing up and down, staring straight ahead.

By the time they reached the church-hospital, it was quite dark. Inside a few candles were burning, their flickering light shining through the stained glass windows.

'You'll find a goodly supply of water here. That's about all,' he said. 'Goodnight, toodly-pip, I'll see you in the morning.'

He got out of the car, gave an order, bowed to the two women, returned to his seat and drove on.

With a pail of water each, the English nurses did the rounds of the crowded church. Wounded and dying men were lying everywhere: on the flagstones, in the private chapels, on top of the tombs of ancient warriors and

131

venerable bishops; one even lay spreadeagled on the holy altar, like a sacrifice to some pagan god.

They found quite a few men past all help, others were in dreadful pain. There was one lad who spoke English; his leg was smashed, blood was pouring from his eyes and nose. Whether it was to impress them, they couldn't tell, but he asked, 'Please tell me, when will I be fit enough to return to my unit?'

Another, on discovering that they were from England, painfully turned his back, dragging half his torn leg with him. But almost all the others were grateful to their enemy's nurses, squeezed their hands and smiled warmly.

As for Bea and Floss, they quickly forgot these were German soldiers; they were just poor suffering victims of the war—perhaps shot with one of Doss's shells? thought Floss guiltily.

The odd thing was that the wounded weren't so much concerned with taking a drink as with washing the blood and dirt off hands and face. So for most of the night, they went round with their buckets of water, trying to clean up the wounded, turning muddy blood-caked bodies into some semblance of human beings.

In the morning a German sergeant came in and, after a lot of ritual stamping about, saluted the English nurses. Then he read from a piece of paper, 'I'm to thank you very much from my commanding officer. Supplies arrive this morning. When the lorries are emptied, they will take the wounded to a railhead about ten kilometres behind the lines. Would you please take charge of getting the wounded on to the lorries?'

In a tired voice, Bea replied, 'I'm sure we can manage it. But first we require a bath and something to eat.'

The man did not understand. So she pointed to her mouth and chewed invisible bread, then made washing motions with her hands, singing 'This is the way we wash our hands, wash our hands, wash our hands . . . '

'*Ja, ja, natürlich, meine Dame*,' he said, clicking his heels.

He beckoned them to follow him out of the church to the canteen. The food was awful. They were handed a billy can with two jacket potatoes, a finger of black bread that tasted of turnips, bitter acorn-flavoured coffee and a bowl of turnip cooking water.

As they were sitting alone in one corner eating, a group of grizzled veterans sat down to eat at the same table. Once they learned the two women were English, they began to vent their anger on them. One of the men translated.

'You are all bloody *Schweinehunde*. It's due to you we have no proper food. You won't allow food into the country, so our wives and children are starving; no food, no soap, no fats.'

True, the men looked haggard with gaunt hollow cheeks and the haunted eyes of the starving. Floss and Bea swallowed the food as quickly as they could, then made their exit behind the sergeant. He took them to the men's latrines.

Then, with guards at both ends to keep out prying eyes, they refreshed themselves as best they could without soap or warm water.

All that day they helped the walking wounded on to the trucks. About midday a familiar sight cheered them up: the Millicent Sutherland Red Cross Ambulance drew up at the church—without its cargo of medical supplies. All that traipsing about for nothing!

After work, they were given leave to retrieve their personal belongings—make-up, money, the precious 'Millicent Sutherland passport'.

Around five, the monocled officer strutted up, tapping the cane against his shiny boots.

'I wonder if you ladies would kindly join me for tiffin?'
he said in his affected English.

Gratefully, they followed him to the Kommandant's
office. Over tea, he casually said, 'We are permitted to
keep POWs close to the front to help with the wounded.
There's a hospital just opened about four miles down the
line; I'd like you to serve there with our German Red
Cross.'

No amount of protest made any difference. When they
played their trump card—the passport-letter—he laughed
so hard, the tears ran down his face.

'Dear old Millicent. How is her ladyship? I downed
many a glass of champers with her before the war in
Dresden.'

His grey eyes grew serious.

'Look, it isn't safe for you to return. You have no way
of crossing the front line. In any case, the new hospital
has a ward set aside for English wounded, so you can care
for them as well. What do you say?'

'If we can take our ambulance with us,' said Bea
stubbornly.

He nodded grudgingly.

So they became honorary German nurses.

23

Stretcher to stretcher still they came,
Young and old all looked the same—
Grimed and battered
Bleeding and shattered
And who they were hardly mattered . . .

Remnants of lives and forever lost days,
Families ended, minds that were dazed,
Clutched to the breast
Was all they had left
Of life that had gone and homes that were wrecked. . . .
from 'Bomb Incident' by Barbara Catherine Edwards

A week later they drove to the new hospital in style, with a motorcycle escort in front and behind the ambulance. Their only concession to change of sides was to wear nurse's uniform instead of British Army fatigues and tin helmet. But they spurned the *Pickelhaube* or spiked helmet.

'Be it on your own head,' was the monocled officer's parting quip.

The new hospital turned out to be far from new. It was a rambling old chateau aptly named Bellevue, deep in the Picardy countryside. When they saw the inmates they soon realized someone had a warped sense of humour— for *they* were far from being *belle vue*—a 'beautiful sight'.

This was an experimental centre for turning sow's ears into silk purses or, rather, ugly mugs into slightly less ugly mugs.

Patients sent here from all over the front had suffered facial injuries, faces mostly wrecked and mangled by shell splinters. Men could get along without an arm or a leg, but not without a face. So top surgeons had gathered here to put faces back together again. It was a long tedious business. Sometimes as many as a dozen separate operations had to be performed on a single case, with long intervals in between.

An ear, nose, and throat man could create new nostrils so that a soldier could breathe without a nose, could rebuild a gullet so that he could eat, could insert a plate in a shattered palate, so that he could speak.

An eye surgeon would be needed if his sight could be saved or, where it could not, to trim and clean the empty sockets or create a new one to receive a glass eye.

Most delicate of all was the work entailed in rebuilding a shattered jaw and, where part of the jawbone had gone completely, inserting a bridge of teeth and wire.

Nothing like this had ever been done before; there had been no need, on either side. Now the medical profession was faced with difficult dilemmas. How could a man be sent out to meet the world when all that remained of his face was one eye, one ear, the remnants of a lipless mouth and two small holes that represented nostrils, but in no way looked like a nose?

How could relatives, wives, children, fiancées be expected not to recoil in horror from a monster whose only recognizable feature was the colour of his hair?

In the hospital, at least, they were steeled to such sights. There was one golden rule for staff, as the German Sister explained to Floss and Bea in good English:

'*Always* look a man straight in the face. That's our Golden Rule. Remember, he's watching *your* face to see *your* reaction.'

That was easier said than done, as they soon discovered.

It was simpler to smile, to look a man straight in the face when doing a dressing *before* the wound had healed. Hideous though it was, in a raw, bleeding state, it was not much worse than similar wounds on an arm, leg, stomach, or back.

But the real difficulty arose later when the wounds had healed, when the surgeons had done their best, when soon the man would be discharged from hospital, and he was still a monster. Then, when one searching eye watched keenly for a nurse's reaction, it was hard for her not to drop her eyes in pity.

Some of the German nurses were fresh out of school with little medical training; several soon wilted under the strain. But Floss and Bea, with their experience, quickly gained a reputation for their natural easy manner with the disfigured.

There was a young man with one side of his face blown away. The skin had grown over it, but he was still bandaged. Floss was instructed to syringe his face, but *not* to talk to him—he hated the British, blaming them for his terrible injuries.

While Floss was taking off the dressing she smiled comfortingly at him, patting his arm; he muttered something to her in German. She shrugged her shoulders, smiling all the while. All at once, his body grew rigid and he hissed in English, 'You're English.'

There was no point in denying it. Uncertainly, she murmured 'Yes'.

He fixed her with his one good eye for a moment. His face muscles worked, but no sound emerged. At last, he got out, 'What are you smiling at?'

She smiled gently, saying, 'I'm not smiling *at* you, I'm smiling *to* you.'

That smile must have overcome his feelings; it obviously meant a lot to him because after that he often asked for '*Die englische Fräulein*'. It turned out that before the war he had been a barber in London. 'When I'm better I'll cut your hair,' he promised.

One evening he fished out a book of English fairy tales from under his pillow and asked Floss to read him a story. When she saw the title, she got a fright: 'Beauty and the Beast'. But she read to him quietly. A trickle of tears ran from his good eye when she read, 'And Beauty said to the Beast: "Your ugly shape is not your doing: true beauty lies within, not in what is without." And she put her slender arms about his neck and kissed him tenderly.'

When he later asked her to write a few words in his autograph book, she wrote: 'To a dear friend, Helmut. Always remember: true beauty lies within.'

And when it was time for him to leave, she broke the nurses' rule by putting her arms about his neck and kissing him on the cheek. As she watched him go, she felt there was a certain spring to his step that would help him overcome the trials ahead.

After Floss and Bea had worked at the hospital for a few months, Sister told them that a batch of Allied wounded would be arriving next day.

'Are they disfigured too?' asked Bea.

'Oh no, most have only slight wounds. They're here to help out. It is a decision by some *Dummkopf* up top that English prisoners should be made to see the terrible wounds they've caused.'

Over the months they had grown fond of Sister Brunhilde. Surprisingly, despite their different backgrounds, they seemed to have a lot in common. She told them of life at home in Berlin: German women were driving the yellow postal vans, delivering letters, operating the railways, working lathes in factories, in short, doing their bit for the war effort.

It annoyed her that 'Our working women earn only half the wages normally paid to men for the same work.'

She also told them secretly of strikes and protests against the war, often led by women.

'In April last year, the socialist leader Rosa Luxemburg and her comrade Karl Liebknecht called a May Day demonstration on Potsdamerplatz, demanding "Bread", "Freedom", and "Peace". When they cried "Down with the War!", the police charged through the crowd swinging their sabres to arrest Rosa and Karl. They were both thrown into jail, but the fight goes on!'

In turn, the two English nurses would tell her of Sylvia Pankhurst and others fighting for peace at home.

The British POWs were to be housed in the stables which Floss and Bea had been allowed to make as homely as possible. The horses had long since gone to war or been minced down to sausage meat and bone meal.

The first snow of winter carpeted the cobblestones of the chateau courtyard as two trucks rumbled to a halt outside the stables. German guards let down the tailboards and, to cries of ''Raus! 'Raus! 'Raus!', started roughly pulling the wounded out of the lorries.

But Floss and Bea quickly elbowed their way to the front and took charge.

'Come on, lads,' cried Floss. 'You're in good hands now.'

'Flippin' Ada,' exclaimed one man. 'An angel sent from heaven.'

'No,' said Floss with a laugh. 'From Portsmouth, duckie.'

Someone called back inside the truck, 'Hey, Pompey, there's a lass from your home town here.'

They made way for a young man who limped painfully to the tailboard. When he caught sight of the nurse he almost fell out of the truck.

'Sis!'

'Jack!'

24

Your battle-wounds are scars upon my heart,
Received when in that grand and tragic 'show'
*   You played your part*
*   Two years ago,*

And silver in the summer morning sun
I see the symbol of your courage glow—
*   That Cross you won*
*   Two years ago . . .*

May you endure to lead the Last Advance
And with your men pursue the flying foe
*   As once in France*
*   Two years ago.*

from 'To My Brother' by Vera Brittain

War was full of surprises. None more so than the chance meeting of brother and sister behind enemy lines. She told her story and he his:

'I finished up in a field hospital for an op. While my foot was recovering, we heard the battle coming closer and had to evacuate the hospital in a hurry. The runners ran, the walking wounded walked, and the limpers like me limped—but not far or fast enough. I got nabbed by Jerry and stuck in a wire cage, fed on nothing but mangold-wurzels and got treated rotten—many died in that cage, from either dysentery or starvation. So here I am, sis.'

'Do you remember the final words of your last letter?'

she asked. 'You said you hoped you'd end up in my care. So you've got your wish.'

But the pleasure of sister meeting brother was soon soured by the cruel treatment of the prisoners. A new Kommandant arrived to take charge of the hospital, an old sweat with one eye and a deep purple scar down one side of his face. He took delight in working the prisoners like slaves. They had to act as orderlies—setting trays, dishing out meals, emptying bedpans, washing and shaving the helpless, humping the daily baskets of dirty linen to the laundry.

Once that daily chore was over, they were made to toil in the stone quarry behind the chateau. It was back-breaking work in the cold of winter, amidst snow and slush, and with no decent food to sustain them.

Floss and Bea did what they could to smuggle out loaves of bread and bacon fat, but that didn't go far among forty men.

It wasn't simply the physical side. Patients were also egged on to maltreat the prisoners. Each day, the one-eyed Kommandant had a roll call of prisoners on the wards, followed by screams and curses:

'You fired the gun that ruined this man's face!'

'You ripped his eye out!'

'He can't face his wife and children because of you!'

By whipping up hatred of the prisoners, he made their lives unbearable.

One day, as Jack was helping Floss to load her tray, he whispered urgently, 'I can't stand it any more. I'm gonna make a break for it.'

Floss looked at him in horror.

'You can't, Jack. They'd shoot you down before you got far. The roads are swarming with Germans.'

'I don't care. Death is better than slavery.'

She forced him to promise he wouldn't do anything silly until she'd had a chance to think about it.

An idea began to form in her mind. She wasn't going to be able to dissuade her brother; and without aid he'd be killed for sure. How would Mum take that? There was a slight chance she might be able to help him escape.

Once a month either she or Bea had to drive the ambulance to St Quentin for fresh supplies. Of course, they always had an escort. To make doubly sure, one of the two nurses had to remain behind 'as hostage' in case the other tried to escape.

A couple of days later, she told Jack her plan.

'On Sunday, it's my turn to do the supplies run. Now, the front line is only about six miles from here. If I can get rid of my outriders and hide you inside the ambulance, we might make it.'

It was agreed. She told no one of her plan, not even Bea. Jack was to hide in a dirty linen basket late on Saturday night; early next morning before daybreak, Floss would get two night porters to help her load the basket into the back of the van.

It was done, not without the porters' grumbles and curses at the weight.

The only guarded part of the chateau was the stables housing the POWs, so she expected no trouble as she drove out quietly. Since the escort wasn't due till eight, the same time as the POW roll call, she had two hours before the alarm went up.

Direction was no problem, as the boom-boom of shells and guns was better than any compass. Once on the road, however, Floss began to count the many obstacles they were up against.

First the German patrols.

Second the motorbike pursuit once the balloon went up.

143

Third the gauntlet of British and German gunfire.

Then, what if she made it that far? If she didn't return, they'd shoot Bea. If she did return, they'd shoot her for helping a prisoner to escape. She could expect no less a punishment than Edith Cavell got.

What a pickle!

For the moment, her first trial lay ahead at the road block. As she pulled over, the sleepy sentry came out of his hut to inspect her papers. He'd seen her a few times before, but seeing no motorbike escort, he shouted a question, making riding movements with his fists, and blowing out his lips: 'Brrrmm, Brrrmm.'

She smiled gently and put her two hands to her cheek, saying 'Asleep'.

'Ach, schlaffen,' he said with a sympathetic grin, handing back her papers and raising the boom.

The next patrol was more suspicious, demanding a proper search of the vehicle. Floss watched the two men, heart in mouth. One of them tapped the laundry basket with his stick.

'Was ist dass?'

She said the first word that came into her head, 'Lice.'

And she made walking signs with her fingers up her arm.

'Vermin, creepy-crawlies, pests.'

The message seemed to get through and he moved rapidly away from the basket, scratching himself automatically.

She drove on, turning off the main road on to a lane that she vaguely recalled when skirting the German sector of the battlefield with the monocled officer. With any luck, it might bring them out to the abandoned trench system and then . . . the British-held town of Péronne.

So it turned out, but not before several scary moments as she had to bluff her way through a German foot patrol, making signs of carrying stretchers for wounded men.

More than once the wheels got stuck in holes and ditches, and Jack had to leave his hiding place to shove and tug.

Finally, when they appeared to be in No Man's Land, he sat up front next to his sister. He had become his own cheery self again as he saw freedom coming closer.

'We've made it, Flo. My clever little sister.'

He hugged and kissed her. But her words wiped the smile off his face.

'I'm going back.'

'But you can't,' he cried. 'They'll shoot you.'

'Maybe.' She sighed. 'But I can't let Bea down or betray Sister's trust. And then there's my patients.'

'But they're Germans,' he objected.

'Jack, dear,' she said slowly, 'I've been thinking over Edith Cavell's last words: "It isn't enough to love one's own people. I must have no hatred or bitterness towards anyone." That wise woman had grasped a great truth and risen above hatred for the enemy. The warmongers back home made her a heroine, preferring to ignore her last message; in their lust for war, they used her to fan the flames of the hatred she herself had overcome. I must follow her example.'

Jack was silent. Although he would gladly give up his life for his sister, nothing he said would change her mind. And there was something else: in his heart of hearts he knew she was right.

They drove across the bleak landscape of No Man's Land in utter silence. The guns were quiet this Sunday morning, as if in sympathy with the sad parting.

'Greater love hath no man than this,' murmured Jack, recalling his scripture lessons, 'that a sister should lay down her life for her brother.'

'Don't be soppy,' she snapped. 'We could both still be blown to Kingdom Come if they don't see our Red Cross markings. Anyway, I've no intention of laying down my life. Not me! I'm too young to die. I've got plans to win the vote, train to be a doctor, I might even become the first prime minister in petticoats. How about that then?'

Her attempts to lift the gloom were suddenly cut short by a dusty furrow ploughed in the track before them, and the sound of a swarm of mosquitoes about their ears.

'That Tommy's as blind as a bat,' snorted Jack.

And, standing up in his seat, he shouted at the top of his voice, 'Hold your fire! We're English!'

The bellow had its effect.

'Name, number, and rank,' a voice bawled back.

'Typical,' muttered Jack. 'Bullets first, ask questions second . . .'

In a loud voice, he cried, 'Loveless, J. 872563. Private, Royal Hampshire Regiment. Anyone would think,' he exploded, 'they have a check list. Jesus wept!'

'Proceed with caution,' a shout rolled over the hundred yards of dead space.

Jack and Floss could clearly see the English trenches—and a hundred rifles trained on the ambulance. It would take only one trigger-happy twit to put a bullet in them.

Fortunately, as Floss wove a zigzag path through barbed wire and shell holes, the waiting soldiers recognized the red and white markings on the vehicle's sides. A young officer put his head above the parapet, and a gloved hand pointed to a makeshift bridge of duckboards flung across the dug-out.

As soon as the ambulance was safely behind the lines, he ordered men to surround it—just in case it was a cunning plot, a Wooden Horse full of Huns eager to catch them unawares. But a quick glance inside and underneath the vehicle was proof that the only occupants were the private and the nurse.

That seemed to lift the tension and, as Floss helped Jack to the ground, an odd sound broke out behind them. It was the young officer: taking out his spotted handkerchief and waving it in the air, he shouted out, 'Three cheers for the plucky nurse and English soldier. Hip-hip, hoorah, hip-hip, hoorah, hip-hip, hoorah! That's one in the eye for Jerry,' he cried, obviously excited at the gallant escape from German hands. 'I shall recommend you for an award.'

'I'm going back,' said Floss bluntly.

Her words bowled him over. It was beyond his understanding.

'Balderdash, Nurse. I won't allow it,' he exclaimed.

Jack quickly jumped in, afraid his sister would start spouting about loyalty to Germans.

'My sister is caught in a tragic dilemma, sir. If she doesn't go back, her English colleague will be shot. So this brave young woman has volunteered to return, at great risk to her own life, to help her fellow nurse and other POWs to escape.'

Jack squeezed his sister's hand to keep her quiet. He knew she hated lies, even to save her own life.

The major hummed and hawed. Finally, inspired by the derring-do of this gallant English nurse, he gave permission for the return journey.

'Best of luck, sis,' said Jack in parting. 'When we get home I'll reward you with my football boots.'

His attempt at a smile went all wrong: the watery eyes and twitching cheekbones were too strong to let the sun come out. To hide his tears, he hugged her tight; as he buried his face in her hair, she felt warm drops fall on her neck.

'Have that foot seen to,' she commanded in her best

matronly voice; 'and build up that skinny frame, otherwise Mum'll think the army doesn't look after its men. Write and tell the family . . . let the duchess know.'

She tore herself away, climbed up to her seat and swiftly drove across the duckboards. As she turned back to wave goodbye, everyone, as one man, stood above the trenches, clapping and waving their hands. All at once, a deep voice rang out, 'Fare ye well, ma bonny lass!'

She recognized it at once: it was the Scots sergeant who'd sung 'Annie Laurie' for her. He now stood to attention on the edge of the parapet and sang out loud and clear,

'There's a rose that grows in No Man's Land,
And it's wonderful to see.
Tho' it's sprayed with tears,
It will live for years
In my garden of memory.
It's the one red rose
The soldier knows,
It's the work of the Master's Hand;
In the War's great curse stands the Red Cross Nurse,
She's the Rose of No Man's Land.'

Floss thought that war had hardened her to everything, but that song for her moved her to tears. In the stillness of that December morning, the sounds must have carried across the divide all the way to the German trenches. For as she approached the German line, she could hardly credit her eyes—men were standing up and clapping her, crying out, *'Hier kommt die englische Rose!'*

Then, all at once, a red-faced Bavarian sergeant sang out, 'She's de Rose off No Man's Land!'

If only they knew she had smuggled out an English prisoner from right under their noses, they might well have dubbed her deadly nightshade instead of rose!

148

She had little difficulty returning the way she'd come two hours before; the patrols didn't even bother to search the ambulance. It was only when her delayed escort came roaring down the road that her troubles began. To say that they were staggered to see her was an understatement. They almost fell off their motor bikes in amazement.

Relieved to have their prey, the four outriders fell in before and behind, as if to show they had the flying ambulance well and truly cornered.

When she rattled over the familiar courtyard cobblestones, she saw that another welcoming party was waiting to greet her—though without applause or singing. Their faces were distinctly stony.

The roll had been called, and Jack's absence resulted in all hell being let loose. Kommandant Lämmer naturally thought he'd lost a prisoner, a nurse, and an ambulance. His one good eye blazed and his purple scar throbbed like some raw pulse.

He had had poor Bea dragged out of bed, interrogated, then thrown into the old wine cellar under lock and key.

The surprising return of two-thirds of the quarry hardly improved his temper. Through an interpreter he demanded to know what had happened to the prisoner. She saw no point in lying. As she sat across the table, hands tied behind her back, she felt calm and content: she'd done her duty and Jack was safe; it didn't matter what they did to her.

'I drove him to English lines,' she said boldly.

His one eyebrow shot up in surprise, but he continued to rant and rage.

'You will be shot. That is the punishment for helping a prisoner to rejoin Allied forces.'

She stood her ground, looked him straight in the eye

and said quietly, 'He is wounded. He cannot fight. I helped him gain better treatment than you allowed him here.'

'You will be shot!' he repeated. 'I will make sure of that.'

25

It is spring.
The buds break softly, silently.
This evening
The air is pink with the low sun,
And birds sing.

Do we believe
Men are now killing, dying—
This evening,
While the sky is pink with the low sun,
And birds sing?
No . . .

So they go on killing, dying,
This evening,
And through summer, autumn, winter,
And through spring.

'Spring 1917' by Beatrice Mayor

Before she was led off, Floss made an appeal for Bea.

'All that I did, I did alone. Nurse Norton knew nothing of it. She is totally innocent.'

The Kommandant was unimpressed.

He felt sure they were in cahoots. True, they could have made the escape attempt together: the fact that one stayed behind and the other had returned to save her friend did point to Bea's innocence. But he smelt a rat . . .

'The Military Tribunal will decide that,' he barked. 'Take her away and lock her up.'

Since the chateau had only one wine cellar, Floss had to be left to stew in the vine juice with Bea. The wine vaults may have smelt deliciously of fruity wine, but they were freezing cold and dingy like dungeons; the only light filtered in from two inches of barred window at ground level.

Bea was baffled to see her friend.

'I say, Florence, what in Heaven's name are you doing here? I heard you'd made a break for it. Did the rotters catch you?'

'No, I missed your company, old dear,' said Floss with a laugh.

'Ah well,' sighed Bea, 'what say we celebrate our reunion with a bottle of champers? And you can tell me all about it.'

The popping cork startled the guard outside the cellar door; but once he'd ensured it wasn't a gunshot, he licked his lips and let the condemned women enjoy their last drink.

As they took turns swigging the bottle of vintage champagne, Floss related her story. At the end, Bea took her large chilly hand in hers and was clearly overcome— as much from bubbly as from gratitude.

'Dashed good of you, Florence,' she muttered, a tear in her eye.

The other protested.

'Oh no, I'm no martyr, Bea. To tell the truth you weren't my only consideration. There's Sister Brunhilde; she's a decent sort, one of us really, and she'd have got it in the neck if one of her nurses had skedaddled. Then, well, I'm not sure how to put it . . . You see, I've grown quite fond of my patients. How would *they* feel knowing I'd run off and left them in the lurch?'

Bea was silent, wondering whether she'd have had such courage. After a while, she looked up and said cheerily,

'Anyway, chin up, old bean. You wait till Her Grace learns of this pickle we're in. She'll pull out all the stops, pull a few strings and get us out of here in no time.'

Floss wasn't so optimistic, recalling the monocled officer's fit of the giggles at the mere mention of the duchess.

Later that day, they heard a car draw up outside their low window, then heavy steps clattering down the stone steps to the cellar. All at once, the door flew open and in marched Kommandant Lämmer with a small, well-dressed man in civvies.

He introduced himself as Military Prosecutor Herr Stöber.

A far-off bell rang in Floss's head: 'Stöber', 'Stöber' . . .

Of course! This was the man who had sent Nurse Cavell to her doom!

'The notorious Herr Stöber,' exclaimed Floss. 'The man who specializes in executing English nurses.'

No flicker of emotion showed in his face, neither resentment, nor pleasure.

'I do my job,' he said coldly in good English. 'You plainly hold me responsible for Nurse Cavell's execution. May I remind you it was the Military Tribunal in Brussels that sentenced her to death. What is more, she condemned herself out of her own mouth.'

With that, he stood aside as two guards, at a sign from the Kommandant, prodded the two women out of the cellar and up the steps. They were quickly bundled into the back seat of a long black limousine. Herr Stöber took the front seat, next to the driver.

And off the car drove the short distance to St Quentin.

This time it was not the old Gothic church that was their destination, but a sinister grey fortress: the prison of St Etienne perched on a hill above the town, like an eagle staring down from its eyrie. Its high walls were a constant reminder to the townspeople of their cruel German masters, for though many French patriots had gone in, few had ever come out alive.

Floss and Bea were put in different cells, six foot by nine, stone cold and lit only by a flickering gas flame. Along one side was an iron bedstead with a pewter pot beneath it. No toilet, no wash basin, not even daylight. Just grey stone floor, grey stone walls, grey stone ceiling, and a low iron door.

So began days and nights of cold, hunger, and solitude. Each morning a male warder led them down a dark passage, with cells on either side, out into the tiny women's courtyard; it reminded Floss of a skittle alley. It had an old water pump in one corner and a stinking sewer in the other.

They had to wash in the freezing water from the pump—no soap or towel—and empty their pots into the open sewer.

No talking was permitted.

On the tenth day, they were taken straight from the yard, without warning, to a dim stuffy room in another part of the prison. A familiar natty figure awaited them: Herr Stöber. He was as brisk and polite as ever, informing them that their case would be heard that morning at ten.

'You will please wait here until you are summoned. No talking.'

The two women exchanged anxious glances. Both thought how the other had aged in the ten-day confinement; they longed to chat, hold hands for comfort, offer words of hope. After all, this could be their last day on earth.

At least they didn't have to agree on their stories: all they had to do was tell the truth.

Dead on the stroke of ten, the courtroom doors opened and an officer, their interpreter, beckoned them into the high-ceilinged, oak-panelled courtroom. On a dais at the far end sat the three-man tribunal, all high-ranking officers in uniform. The President in the centre wore the Iron Cross.

In the well of the court sat a typist before a large new typewriting machine; and on either side of her, like two stone pillars, stood armed guards.

That was all. No defence lawyer. No witnesses. No public gallery.

First in the dock was Bea. They did not detain her long. She wasn't the big fish they had caught. The evidence before the court clearly showed she was innocent. All she had to do was verify her statement. Although Herr Stöber tried to trip her up, she stuck to her guns and was soon asked to stand down.

Before they came to their main prize, the three officers took a break, evidently to agree the verdict on Bea. On their return, the President announced solemnly, 'Not guilty. Cleared on all counts.'

She was free to go.

As she squeezed past Floss, Bea quickly leant over and kissed her cheek. No words were necessary.

'Nurse Florence Loveless!'

This was it. How vividly she recalled the story of Edith Cavell.

She took her place in the dock, confirmed her name and position at the hospital.

Herr Stöber rose, adjusted his tie and began to read out the evidence. It was damning.

'Private Jack Loveless, a POW employed at the hospital, is the accused's brother. In the early hours of the morning of Sunday 13 December 1917, the accused wilfully concealed her brother in a linen basket at the back of her Red Cross ambulance. She tricked her way through German lines, using the Red Cross as cover, so enabling Private Loveless to reach Allied lines.'

155

The President peered down at her over his steel-rimmed glasses.

'Is that so?' he asked drily.

Floss nodded.

'Is that so?' she was asked again, more sternly this time.

'Yes, it is,' she said nervously. 'But it is not the whole story . . .'

The President ignored her and nodded to the Military Prosecutor to continue.

'By the rules of war, anyone found guilty of treason shall be shot. It is beyond doubt that the prisoner aided and abetted the escape of a prisoner of war, thereby enabling him to rejoin the war against our forces.

'I therefore submit that the accused, Nurse Florence Loveless, is guilty of treason.'

He sat down, his task done.

Floss was alone. There was no one to help or advise her. Her fate hung by the thread she had to weave herself. What was she to say? It could only be the truth; she was incapable of telling lies.

She surprised the court by starting in German. She quoted the words from the First Epistle to St John, printed above a picture hanging in Sister Brunhilde's office. The painting showed an angel resting a laurel wreath on a fallen soldier.

'*Wir sollen auch unser Leben für die Brüder lassen.* We must also lay down our lives for our brothers. If I must die, then I am happy to die for my brother. That I helped him escape from captivity is beyond dispute. That I used a Red Cross ambulance to smuggle him through German lines is also true. If that is treason, I stand guilty and must pay the price. I would only say two things in my defence.

'First, my brother was wounded, his foot smashed. He was denied treatment at our hospital—by order of the

Kommandant. It is totally untrue that I enabled him to rejoin the war, for he is an invalid and "out of combat". Second, you will be aware that I could have escaped myself. I did not do so because I would not endanger my friend Nurse Norton. But there was another reason.'

She paused and took a deep breath, unsure how to explain to these unforgiving men.

'You see, a nurse's duty is above all to her patients. She is their hope and comfort. As such she owes loyalty to no nation or battle cause, solely to healing the sick. May I quote to you the last words of Nurse Edith Cavell—whom you shot for treason on 12 October 1915: "I realize that patriotism is not enough. I must have no hatred or bitterness towards anyone." That noble woman had no hatred even for those who murdered her . . . '

She stopped briefly, looking first at Herr Stöber, then at the three officers, wondering if they would understand.

'Nurse Cavell rose above patriotism. All she thought about was her patients—whether English, French, or German. Nationality does not count. I share that belief. I love Germans no less than English in my care. It is an honour to serve humanity.'

She stood back, hands clasped before her, head bowed. She felt at peace with herself and the world. She'd had her say. What happened now was out of her hands.

After the translation, there was an awkward silence in the courtroom, broken only by the tap-tap-tap of the typist recording every word.

It was only when the President rose that the two guards snapped to attention, breaking the awkward hush with the clicking of their heels. The three officers were about to leave the courtroom when the doors suddenly opened and an elderly man entered. It was the prison governor.

He made his way nervously to the front of the court and whispered urgently to the President who had to lean forward to catch the message. After a while, the President straightened up and announced, with an apologetic glance at the prosecutor, 'Apparently, witnesses for the defence have arrived. This is most irregular, but I must admit them.'

Waving a hand impatiently to the governor, he indicated both his annoyance and his resignation.

Floss was puzzled. Who on earth could be risking their neck for her sake? She was astonished when two familiar figures entered the court.

The first was a tall grey-haired woman in the dark blue uniform of the German nursing corps. She strode purposefully to the front of the court and stated her name clearly:

'Sister Brunhilde Pohl, chief nursing officer at the 625th Sanitäts Hospital.'

The second was a soldier, frail and so badly disfigured that none of the officers could bear more than a brief glance at his face. He limped slowly and painfully to the base of the dais to give his name,

'Unterfeldwebel Helmut Werner.'

Floss was overcome with emotion at this unexpected intervention. That Sister Brunhilde should testify on her behalf was moving enough. But that this German veteran who had once hated all English people should try to save her life was beyond belief.

They gave their evidence in untranslated German. But it was obvious from Sister Brunhilde's manner that she had more sympathy with the prisoner than with the men in court. Even Herr Stöber, who initially dismissed her with a sneer, was affected by her withering contempt for him. Whatever it was she said she certainly wiped the smug expressions off the faces of the officers.

Nor did they enjoy the quiet, slurred words of the disabled staff sergeant. If the effect of Sister's testimony resembled a rifle butt, his was a bayonet, piercing their guard time and again.

No greater proof was needed for Floss's claim that she loved Germans no less than English in her care. And it seemed her German colleague and former patient felt the same.

The two witnesses were politely thanked for their time and duly dismissed. As she passed, Sister Brunhilde gave her a cheery smile and broad wink. It was hard to tell from the man's disfigured face what his feelings were; but the snip-snip sign with his fingers reminded her of his promise to cut her hair once the war was over.

Floss felt so much better. Whatever they did to her now, she knew that her faith in humanity had been justified.

26

Whom shall we blame for the folly of war?
Whom shall we tell these stories for?
Who will believe
The sadness of death,
The terror, the fear, and the emptiness—
What can they know
Of the vacant eyes
The sorrow too deep
In the heart that dies?

from 'Bomb Incident' by Barbara Catherine Edwards

In the cosy annexe behind the courtroom, the three officers lit up cigars and sat back contentedly in the deep leather armchairs. No one spoke: there was nothing to say. They had made up their minds ten days previously. For appearance's sake they had had to put on the courtroom charade.

Let no one say German justice was not fair, even in wartime.

Their sole concern had been Law and Order.

The accused had broken the Law; she had committed a treasonable act and had to be punished. The sentence for treason was death.

The accused had violated Order; she had helped a prisoner escape and had to be seen to be punished. Order had to be restored—through death by firing squad.

After finishing their cigars, the three Law and Order officers stubbed them out without a word, brushed ash and

160

creases from their uniforms and filed solemnly back into court.

They were wearing their caps.

The President did not sit down. Flanked by his two grim-faced colleagues, he read out the brief sentence.

'Mademoiselle Florence Loveless is found guilty of treason. She is to be executed by firing squad at dawn.'

There was an awful hush. Even the typist held her breath. Herr Stöber permitted himself a fleeting smile: he was always proud of a job well done.

The condemned prisoner stood in the dock, unable to take in the translated words. A flood of thoughts overwhelmed her: of Mum and Doss, Jack and the kids, Bea and Sister Brunhilde, her patients . . . Yet the words that hammered away inside her numb mind were:

'But tomorrow's Christmas Day!'

She was to be shot on Christmas Day!

It was a relief to be back alone in her cell. As the sediment of doubt gradually settled on the floor of her mind, her thoughts grew clear and uncluttered.

'How long do I have?'

By the darkening windows of the court she guessed it was early evening, around six or half past.

'Only twelve hours left.'

Just then she caught the faint chiming of distant church bells—counting down the hours for Christmas Eve mass. It was the church where she had first tended enemy wounded. She had no regrets.

Her peace was suddenly disturbed by the French warder, bringing in her last supper: a tepid turnip soup and chunk of dry brown bread that tasted of sawdust.

The man had been told to ask if she wished to see the prison chaplain—at least that is what she understood by him drawing the sign of the cross in the air and pointing down the passageway.

'No thank you,' she said firmly. 'But I'd like pen and paper.'

She made writing signs.

'*Ah, papier pour écrire . . . Attends, mademoiselle, attends.*'

He went out, locking the door behind him; ten minutes later he returned with a pencil and single sheet of paper.

'*Voilà. C'est tout ce qu'on est permis . . .*'

He gave an apologetic shrug.

'*Merci, monsieur,*' she said as he left her to her letter writing.

So much to say: only one sheet of paper.

To whom should she write? Doss, Jack, Bea, Duchess of Sutherland? No, it could only be Mum.

She sat on the edge of the bed, with the sheet of paper on her lap.

St Etienne Prison   Christmas Eve 1917
Dear Mum,
                    I'm writing to you from my prison cell.
They're going to shoot me at dawn. I'm not afraid.
Actually, I feel quite at peace. Then this war has
broken so many hearts; I'm just one of its many
victims.
         Tell Dossie to keep up the good fight until we
get the vote—then we can put a stop to war.
Ask Jack not to worry: I'd do it all over again if
need be.
         If my friend Beatrice Norton contacts you,
please thank her for her friendship and everything.
Put some primroses on Dad's grave for me.
That's all. My paper's run out. Love to you all.

Floss x x x x x x x
PS I don't blame Germans for my death. I blame
    only the war.

She folded the paper in four and banged on her cell door until the warder arrived.

'Please send this letter to England,' she said, thrusting it into his hand. 'Here's the address.'

'*Angleterre? Lettre? Adresse? Entendu, mademoiselle.*'

She could see he was eager to please, evidently moved by her fate.

She was left alone, listening on the hour to her life chiming away. She could not sleep for waiting for the next chime.

Three o'clock.

Four o'clock.

Five o'clock.

Six o'clock . . .

Where were they? Come on. Let's get it over with.

When is it dawn?

'Merry Christmas, Florence!' she wished herself.

She was living on borrowed time.

Seven chimes had barely died away when footsteps echoed down the passageway; they were coming closer and closer. All at once the door opened and three men appeared in the doorway: the French warder, the German Kommandant, and the courtroom interpreter.

No one said a word.

She rose from the bed and followed them down the dim passageway. Despite the early hour, prisoners were at the bars of their cells to wish her well.

'Be brave, little one!'

'Bravo, English!'

'*Vous êtes un ange.* Saint Florence.'

'*Une prière pour vous!*'

Even the warder fumbled for her cold hand and shook it warmly, as if cleansing himself of bloodstained hands.

As she passed down the corridor, she nodded in a daze

to right and left. Her thoughts were more on the practical details of how she would be shot.

Would they shoot her in the prison yard?

Or, like Edith Cavell, would she be taken out of town, out of sight?

That question was soon answered.

They led her through the great iron gates, beyond the high walls into the cold light of day. A car was waiting. This was it.

'Farewell, friends. Farewell, life.'

27

How sweet, how sweet will be the night
When windows that are black and cold
Kindle anew with fires of gold;

When dusk in quiet shall descend
And darkness come once more a friend;

When wings pursue their proper flight
And bring not terror but delight;

When clouds are innocent again
And hide no storms of deadly rain;

When the round sky is swept of wars
And keeps but gentle moon and stars. . . .
from 'How Sweet the Night' by Rachel Bates

Without being told, she slid into the back seat. Only the interpreter sat in the car with her as the driver drove off.

That was odd. She had expected an armed guard—in case she made a dash for it. Nurse Cavell had had a guard. Was she too unimportant?

Some twenty minutes later, as snowflakes began to float down from the gloomy heavens, the car drew up at L'Hôtel de Ville, a once grand town hall, now peppered with bullet holes and commandeered by the German High Command.

So this is where they do their dirty work, she thought grimly. But they can hardly squeeze a battalion of riflemen into the stable yard . . .

But instead of being led out to be blindfolded and stood up against a wall, she was taken up the elegant gilt staircase to what had once been an ornate banqueting room. It was now the headquarters of the German Governor of St Quentin.

He was sitting at a huge desk, a bulky, shaven-headed man with a walrus moustache waxed at the ends. From his grey tunic hung an Iron Cross at the neck and an eight-pointed silver star on the left pocket. His watery, bloodshot eyes fixed her with a look of hatred and contempt.

To one side, in a red plush chair, was the President of the Military Tribunal, sitting to attention.

'*Nehmen Sie Platz!*' the Governor ordered in a voice roughened by a thousand brandies.

'Sit down, please,' said the interpreter quietly behind her.

The Governor heaved his bulk out of the chair and picked up a piece of paper from the desk. He advanced on the condemned nurse, waving the paper angrily and bellowing at her. He talked so fast the interpreter could only translate odd phrases.

'You see this? Telegram from Prince von Bülow . . . our former Chancellor . . . Here, let me read it . . . ''The shooting of Nurse Cavell was an act whose usefulness did not match her moral guilt . . . I learn from an old acquaintance—an English lady of breeding and integrity—that you plan a similar folly. Do *not*, I repeat *not*, make the same mistake.'' '

Floss's spirits rose. Did that mean a reprieve? Had the good old duchess really pulled some strings?

The walrus moustache continued to bounce up and down as the thick lips continued to snarl and curse. All that needed translating was, 'He says you are free to return to the hospital.'

The Governor was still ranting when Floss was escorted from the room and out of the building.

Outside in the falling snow, the German interpreter grasped her hand and shook it warmly.

'Come,' he said, 'before you return to the hospital, let us celebrate your release.'

With a word to the driver, the car drove off and, to Floss's surprise, drew up beside the old church. The cheery sounds of carols floated out into Christmas morning. The interpreter led the way through the wooden doorway into the brightly-lit church.

No wounded soldiers lay in pews or mangers; they had all been evacuated. The church was now full of women, elderly men, and young children.

Floss found herself standing in a back pew between a little pig-tailed French girl and the young German. And when the organ strains of 'Silent Night' resounded through the church, English and German voices sang out with the French.

Never had Floss sung so joyfully.

'Silent Night, Holy Night,
All is calm, all is bright . . . '

Her silent night was over. Her busy day was about to begin.

Bibliography

For inspiration and material from the following:

In Time of War. War Poetry selected by Anne Harvey (Blackie, 1987).

Scars Upon My Heart. Women's Poetry and Verse of the First World War, Catherine W. Reilly (Virago, 1981).

Lyn Macdonald, *The Roses of No Man's Land* (Penguin Books, 1993).

Angela Woollacott, *On Her Their Lives Depend. Munitions Workers in the Great War* (University of California Press, 1994).

Richard van Emden, Steve Humphries, *Veterans. The Last Survivors of the Great War* (Leo Cooper, 1998).

Sarah Peacock, *Votes for Women: the Women's Fight in Portsmouth* (The Portsmouth Papers, 39, 1983).

Sally Grant, *Edith Cavell. Nurse and Heroine* (The Larks Press, 1995).

A. E. Clark-Kennedy, *Edith Cavell* (Faber, 1978).

John Keegan, *The First World War* (Hutchinson, 1998) (for the map of 'The Western Front').

Vera Brittain, *Testament of Youth* (Virago, 1978).

Acknowledgements

Rachel Bates: lines from 'How Sweet the Night' from *Songs from a Lake* (Hutchinson), reprinted by permission of The Random House Group Ltd.

Vera Brittain: extracts from *Testament of Youth* (Victor Gollancz, 1933, Virago, 1978), reprinted by permission of Mark Bostridge and Rebecca Williams, her literary executors, and Victor Gollancz, publisher.

May Wedderburn Cannan: 'When the Vision Dies' originally from *The Splendid Days* (Blackwell, 1917), republished in *The Tears of War* (Cavalcade Books, 2000), reprinted by permission of James C. Slater.

Rose Macaulay: 'Picnic, July 1917', © The Estate of Rose Macaulay, reprinted by permission of PFD on behalf of the Estate of Rose Macaulay.

Beatrice Mayor: 'Spring 1917' from *Poems—1919* (Allen & Unwin), reprinted by permission of HarperCollins Publishers Ltd.

Carola Oman: lines from 'Brussels 1919' from *The Menin Road* (Hodder & Stoughton, 1919), reprinted by permission of Hodder & Stoughton Limited.

Millicent Sutherland: lines from 'One Night' originally published in *Lest We Forget* edited by H. B. Elliott (Jarrolds, 1915), reprinted by permission of Elizabeth, Countess of Sutherland.

Sara Teasdale: 'There Will Come Soft Rains' from *Collected Poems* (Macmillan Inc., 1920) copyright renewed 1948 by Marnie T. Whales, reprinted by permission of Special Collections, Wellesley College, Massachusetts.

Bettina Wegner: 'The Enemy', translated by Agnes Stein, from *Wenn Meine Lieder Nicht Mehr Stimmen*, (1979) reprinted by permission of Bettina Wegner.

Despite attempts to contact copyright holders this was not possible in every case. If notified we will be pleased to rectify any errors or omissions at the earliest opportunity.